TOMMY & MERRY AND THE TWELVE DAYS OF CHRISTMAS

Ellie Hall

Copyright © 2022 by Ellie Hall

All rights reserved.

No part of this book may be reproduced in any form or by any electronic or mechanical means, including information storage and retrieval systems, without written permission from the author, except for the use of brief quotations in a book review.

This is a work of fiction. Names, characters, businesses, places, events, and incidents are either the products of the author's imagination or used in a fictitious manner. Any resemblance to actual persons, living or dead, or actual events is purely coincidental.

For my Nonna

ABOUT THIS BOOK

No matter which way you slice it, pizza and pie are delicious, but love is complicated.

Merry

My lifelong dream is to open a pie shop in my hometown. But because I'm flat broke, to defray the liability, the leasing agent insists I go into business with what's sure to be a pimply pizza boy.

Problem 1: He's more like an Italian Stallion. Problem 2: That tossing action really builds the biceps. Is it hot in here? I'll blame it on the oven. Problem 3: I knew Tommy in college and he still bakes my buns.

Tommy

To reunite my family, I'm opening a pizza place. The catch is I have to share the space with a pie baker. Not going to happen. As a former fireman, I'm all about teamwork, but I'm not sharing the dough.

ABOUT THIS BOOK

Problem 1: Back in college, as a joke, we made a marriage pact. Problem 2: Like a pair of responsible adults, we agreed not to mix business and pleasure. Problem 3: Ten years later, Merry is still a cutie pie.

Merry

With a flurry of orders, twelve families in need, and a pie thief on the loose, it's hard to know if we can crust each other. Trust. That was supposed to be trust each other. I've got pie (and Tommy) on my mind...and heart.

Tommy

Actually, those are the least of our problems. With only twelve days until Christmas, we have to prove to the building owner that we're the best business for the spot or risk losing it to a chain coffee shop...and with all the pressure and stress, we also risk losing each other.

This is book 1 in the Costa Brothers Cozy Christmas Comfort Romance Series, following six single, stubborn, and loyal brothers as they find their happily ever afters. They're clean and wholesome romance, faith-friendly, stand alone stories but are best enjoyed together.

A GIFT FOR YOU

Do you love sweet, swoony romance?
Stories with happy endings?
Falling in love?

New Year with a Billionaire, a sweet second chance romance with Italian flavor!
Visit EllieHallAuthor.com to get your copy.

PROLOGUE

𝒟ear Santa,
    I know, I know. It's been a while. I'm also aware that I'm probably too old to be writing to you. Like way too old. But I'm, uh, not sure what else to do. See, I'm hoping to be on your nice list this year. I've been good. Promise. For instance, spending time with my sister has become more bearable because her kids are so cute. Just kidding. I love Nadine and them, of course. Mostly them. Okay, I'll stop now because I'm not helping my case.

If you still send your "helpers" out to check on us good little girls and boys, then you'll know all about the bake-a-thon, the charity work I've been doing, and the mission trip to Ecuador. And that's just this year alone.

Also, I'm sorry for being a brat about the annual pony thing for Christmas. Turns out Nadine made up the story that you were going to get me one. Every year, she'd say that you changed your mind and didn't bring the pony because you didn't like me, claiming I was definitely on the naughty list. What did I ever do? Makes me wonder about her missing stocking that time. Nan blamed the dog. However, the more I think about it, I'm not so sure Toodles was at all interested in the spa and beauty contents. Maybe Nadine was the "brat." If that was you (wink, wink) thanks for having my back.

Anyway, as you likely know, I'm still single. Unattached. Available. Yep. Still flyin' solo over here. Single and ready to mingle. Currently accepting applications.

Wait. Hold up. Santa, don't worry, I'm not suggesting anything between us. I'd never, especially not with Mrs. Claus in the picture. But, you know, if you still prepare the 'ole sleigh, rig up the reindeer or whatever, and make deliveries, I would not freak out if I woke up on Christmas morning to find a cute guy, around my age with thick hair and a cute smile under the tree.

In fact, I'd be forever in your debt. Because the truth is, I'm starting to get lonely. Sure, I have great friends, a hobby I love, a dream I aspire toward, and all that. But I'd like someone to bake cookies for like your significant other does for you after a hard day at the, uh, workshop in the North Pole.

But I digress. Actually, wait. I'd make my significant other pies because that's my thing. I'll even leave one here for you with this note as an act of good faith. I hope you enjoy it and please save a slice for Mrs. Claus. I'd love to know what she thinks.

Okay, I've rambled enough. Time to get ready for my eleventh wedding of the year. Yes, you read that right. Though I accidentally wandered into one so I'm not sure if it counts, but I'm so good at being part of the bridal party, they asked me to pinch-hit for the ceremony because the other bridesmaid was stuck in traffic. Also, one of the weddings was for a pair of dogs. Go figure.

Really, I'll stop now. But I just want to say that it's too bad none of the weddings were mine.

Thanks for all the joy, light, and generosity you spread around the world.

Love,
Merilee (aka Desperately Seeking a Santa of my Own)

CHAPTER 1

MERILEE

*P*ie, don't fail me now. The pies I bake are the best thing I know to win people over, make them happy, and brighten their days. Young, old, nurses, firemen, teachers, family—they've all said that the pies I bake equal love at first bite.

I tilt my head from side to side, wondering if *Love at First Bite* could be the name of my dream pie shop. It's a bit long. Maybe the slogan?

I test it out, "Pies by Merilee: Love at First Bite." Nah. Too clumsy.

Even though it's not yet Christmas Eve, I tiptoe to the living room in case Santa passed out after eating too much of the pie I left for him—believe it or not, that's happened, but not to Santa, at least to my knowledge.

My shoulders droop. Sadly, it sits on the coffee table, fully intact. He didn't take my note either. Feeling foolish, I plop onto the couch, tempted to have a nibble.

Instead, I'll bring it to Hawk Ridge Hollow Helpers Care Home & Senior Center, a place where homemade pie is always appreciated.

I have every detail of my dream pie shop outlined, including my business plan, apron design, stickers, swag—all of it—except the name of the place. It's like the missing piece to a puzzle. I tell myself as soon as I figure out a name, I'll be able to move forward and make it happen.

I gaze toward the Christmas tree. "Santa, if you're listening, I really want that special gift I referred to in my letter, but, uh, if that's too big of an ask, I'll take a name and a storefront for my pie shop."

Obviously, I can't have a successful relationship and run a business at the same time, so I'm good with whatever the Big Guy has time for this year.

I'm also well aware that starting my business requires a significant investment, but I've been saving. Coins mostly. Spare change. But it adds up. Nan had a saying about a penny saved.

And trust me, I'm pretty sure Santa isn't listening, but I figure it can't hurt to ask. Especially not when I've exhausted all other means of meeting that special someone.

Thinking about this some more and seeing as Nadine calls me, "String Cheese, the original *single*-serve snack," now would be the perfect time to open up shop because I don't have too many other responsibilities or a plus-one.

Unless Santa pulls through. Though that's not likely.

I don't even have a date for Cassie's wedding, so there's that. I considered going to the next town over and asking some random guy to accompany me (I'd pay him in pie, really it's that good!) but wimped out.

I'm pretty sure everyone in Hawk Ridge Hollow knows about my commitment issues—not with men because I haven't had too many of them come my way. Rather, I tend to take seasonal jobs, so I can leave town should an opportunity arise—like the bake-a-thon I did on HLTV, charity work with children in the city, and the mission trip to Ecuador. I've also been to Romania and Bangladesh in the past with my church.

Every time, there comes a point when I start to feel attached. Like I could stick around, but I know firsthand how risky that can be. Eventually, I end up back home, dreaming of opening a pie shop. But that would mean staying, committing.

I want it so badly, I can taste it (today, it's apple cinnamon spice). But that doesn't solve my single-pringle problem, so what am I to do? It's a cruel game of *Would you rather...*

There's nothing like attending the eleventh wedding of the year, alone. Granted, *Fur*dinand and Lady Bow Wow did have a few cute guests which got me thinking about adopting a dog of my own, but that's a commitment and could prove challenging with the pie shop on the horizon.

Someday. There are a lot of those in my life.

After I do my makeup—I'm a pro at this point—I gather up the copper-colored floor-length satin bridesmaid's dress and sky-high heels. Cassie and Leon's wedding has a harvest theme, appropriate for the late-November event with the additional accent shades of plum, gray, and dusty rose.

At this point, if the pie thing doesn't work out, I could become a wedding planner. Wouldn't that be ironic? I'd go from being forever the bridesmaid, never the bride, to being forever the wedding planner, never wed.

I sigh, ruffling the wide curls I put in my blonde hair, swipe on lipstick, and slide on my boots. Juggling my bag, the dress, and the wedding gift, I grab the pie to drop off since Santa passed on the deliciousness. I guess he's more of a cookie guy. I'll have to check if the post office still puts out the wooden box for "Letters for Santa" like they did when I was a kid.

As mentioned, I'm getting desperate here. And I know it's silly of me, an adult woman, to write Santa, but what can it hurt?

Clouds hang in the sky, and I won't be surprised if it snows soon. The white stuff already covers the slopes of the Hawk Ridge mountain range. As I drive through the quaint ski resort town I grew up in, as usual, I wonder if I should break free—go somewhere else. Then again, I've tried that and always end up back home. There's a reason skiers and tourists alike flock here year-round.

Hawk Ridge Hollow is like a storybook town with its quaint main street lined with whimsical shops, charming architecture, and a stunning mountain backdrop. Moreover, Christmas is an event here.

Another job prospect is I could do local tours—I'm not a Hawkins (all of them are now happily married), but I know as much about the area as a member of the founding family.

"And here on your right is Mom & Lollipop's. They make the best chocolate. Now we're passing the Hawk & Whistle Pub. Their Bannock bread is amazing. Next, you see the Hawk Post, our general store. Not to be confused with the post office, which is that low brick building on the left."

No sign of Santa's letter box yet, but I'll check back.

I continue my mock tour. "That's the Beanery, where you can get coffee, cocoa, and more. And up ahead is the Hawk Ridge Hollow Resort—your one-stop-shop for everything related to snow sports and winter activities. Ski, snowboard, snowshoe, ice skate, and sled. If that's not your thing, there's also a spa, pool, and numerous event spaces, ballrooms, and reception halls."

That's where I'm headed for Cassie's wedding, but I take a left, passing the town that guidebooks call a cross between one of those mini ceramic Christmas scenes and a Bavarian village.

"Welcome to Hawk Ridge Hollow, and thank you for joining me today." I don't tell my pretend tourists that we're taking a quick detour to the Hawk Ridge Hollow Helpers, a care home and senior center.

I say a little prayer as I enter and pass the photo of Nan on the wall collage featuring residents and regulars over the years.

"Miss Merilee, don't you look lovely today. Did you come to finally take me up on that offer for a date?" asks Clive Hughes, one of the residents.

"Even better, I brought an apple pie with extra cinnamon, your favorite."

"You really do know how to charm a man, Miss Merilee."

If only that were true. "Just be sure to share with everyone. No hogging it this time."

He chuckles, having passed out in the easy chair not long ago with the fork still in his hand. "Okay, fine, but I want an extra big slice."

Margie, one of the care workers, waves at me from behind the welcome station. "My, my now I know why he loves you so much."

I set the pie down on the counter and lean in. "Actually, he had a crush on my grandmother and this happens to be her recipe, so I think his sights are simply set on a slice. Extra big," I add.

"Well, you do look nice today. What's the occasion?" Margie asks.

I swish my lips to the side and a forlorn sigh escapes. "Another wedding. And on that note, I'd better hurry, otherwise, I'll be late."

The sadness in my voice mostly has to do with the fact that even though I still visit Hawk Ridge Hollow Helpers regularly, my favorite person is no longer here.

Also, Santa, Clive is great and all, but I was hoping for interest from someone closer to my age (and not previously in love with my grandmother).

I park behind the Hawk Ridge Hollow Resort and hurry to the bridal suite to get ready with the other girls. Chatter greets me when I enter, and it's like the college dorm all over again.

The sticky scent of hair spray, the disarray, the bubbly gushing, and giggling transport me to a time, just over a decade ago, when I imagined myself in a fancy white dress preparing for my big day.

"There you are. I was starting to worry you were going to

stand me up," Cassie says while admiring her reflection in the mirror.

I'll pretend the comment isn't a little dig at me. Bygones are bygones, the water is under the bridge, the fences are mended, and all that.

"I'm here and I brought something blue for you," I say, pulling out a small gift box and giving it a shake.

"Oh, Merilee, you were always so thoughtful. Remember when she'd bake pies for everyone on the floor? Big weekend at Cossington Dorm." Cassie titters because, as usual, I'm the butt of the joke.

If Cassie was the party girl, I was the house mom. She'd sometimes call me the "Mother Hen," among other things.

The girls cackle and for one painful moment, I feel alone and not because I'm still single. Even though Cassie and the other girls always talked about how we were frie-mily, a combination of friends and family, I've never quite felt included or even liked. More like I'm the weird aunt who bakes pies and has twelve cats.

I internally scold myself for always hoping she'd find a piece of cat fur in her slice—not that we had a cat living in the dorm with us.

It also didn't help that I lost my parents to a car wreck when I was four. I'm forever grateful for Nan and Grampa taking Nadine and me in, but it's hard to commit when, time and time again, the people I love inevitably get taken away.

I also tell myself that I'd better accept my fate, or even better, own it like the pie-baking boss that I am.

Nan and Grampa didn't raise a softie. I could drive the tractor by the time I was ten and helped Grampa stack wood—doing double duty because my sister slacked off. Whether I was outside with him or in the kitchen with Nan, it was often quiet but meaningful work, and I don't regret or resent it. But life without them or a boyfriend is starting to get lonely.

Squaring my shoulders, I present Cassie with the small gift box. "It was such an honor that you chose me as a bridesmaid."

"You are so sweet." Cassie pulls off the ribbon and the lid then frowns. "Oh, uh, a handkerchief?"

Everyone stares at the delicate piece of cloth stitched with blue thread and the letter *C* along with a floral design.

"This was my grandmother's. Her name was Cecilia, a *C*-name like you. I thought you should have it. She carried it with her on her wedding day as part of the old custom for a happy marriage." I recite the rhyme about "Something old, something new, something borrowed..."

"Oh," Cassie repeats. "So thoughtful. Thanks." A slight wrinkle forms across the bridge of her nose then she sets the handkerchief down on the table.

I ignore the unpleasant tickle in my chest and the sudden and intense desire to fade into the wallpaper.

"Time for a new playlist," says Ariana, the maid of honor. She saves what's turning into an awkward record scratch of a moment by turning up the music.

The photographer flits around, capturing Cassie as the rest of the bridal party fawns over her. They talk about their wedding days, receptions, and married life. Before long, we're lined up—Ariana in plum, Melissa in gray, Jill in dusty rose, and me in copper. I can't help but feel a little like the fourth place trophy on display being the only single woman in the group.

"Now that we're all married, we're going to start a club, Cassie," Jill says. "I'm thinking of calling it the *First Wives*. Very VIP, right?" Her voice is so bubbly, I'm afraid she'll pop if she doesn't get Cassie's approval.

None of them bother saying anything encouraging like it'll be my turn next. However, like the trooper I am, I grip my mini bouquet, march down the aisle, smile when I'm supposed to, and pretend my feet don't ache in these high heels.

The ceremony is lovely. I hold back the tears that spike the corners of my eyes. It's so beautiful, moving, and inspiring to see two people come together in this way. I cry at every wedding I attend. Yes, even the one with the dogs.

Truly, I'm happy for Cassie and Leon, but I won't pretend that my heart doesn't hurt a little bit too. Not because Leon and I ever had any interest in each other. In fact, today is my first time meeting him. But here I am, still alone.

If I'm going to stick with my sister's cheese analogy, my dating life is like Swiss. There have been a few solid guys, but mostly, it's filled with holes.

This reminds me to look in my grandmother's recipe box for an apple pie I vaguely recall containing cheddar cheese.

After another round of photos, Ariana and I wait in front of the bathroom door outside the reception hall at the Hawk Ridge Hollow Resort.

She says, "It's big of you to be part of the wedding after everything that happened. I mean, they were making out on your bed." She makes a gagging face. "Ick."

I'd hoped to avoid this topic but braced myself for some mention of it from the moment Cassie invited me to join the bridal party. The comment doesn't do my empty stomach any favors. I should've snuck a nibble of Clive's slice of pie while I had the chance...or I could go for a piece of cheese right now. Swiss, cheddar, whatever.

"If I'd walked in on Cassie making out with *my* guy, I don't think I would've been able to forgive her," Ariana goes on, clearly setting me up to gossip.

Another name they had for me was "House Mouse." Despite my sudden craving for cheese, I won't take the bait and fall into her trap.

My voice is like a kite when I say, "Do you mean Tommy Costa? He wasn't my guy. We were just friends." Best friends. Speaking his name out loud after all this time makes my jaw tremble slightly.

Weird. I must be starved.

She raises and lowers her eyebrows. "Just friends, huh? Everyone thought you were a couple. Cassie said you even had a marriage pact. Is that true?"

I do an awkward shake-nod of my head, trying not to let the memories get too close to the surface.

Satisfied that they're not going to breach like a killer whale, I give a dismissive wave of my hand, and answer, "She must've been thinking of a group of psych majors on campus that were surveying students and trying to get them to take a test to find their perfect match. It was like an old-fashioned matchmaking service combined with an early version of a dating app. They used a quiz along with some kind of algorithm to connect potential couples."

Hopefully, that'll pacify Ariana or an orca will miraculously swim by and I can point and say, *Hey, look at that* to distract her.

Inspired, Tommy and I totally took the test, and big surprise, we were a ninety-eight percent perfect match. Of course, we didn't want that prospect to interfere with our friendship, so we agreed to, um, get married *someday*. A day that's come and long gone.

Ariana elbows me. "Oh, come on. Don't tell me there wasn't a little somethin' there."

"*Pfft.* Tommy and I haven't seen each other since—" Since shortly after I walked in on him and Cassie together.

I tried to play it casual like it didn't matter, but unable to hide my hurt, I rapidly retreated. Our friendship faded when I didn't answer his texts or calls. I felt betrayed, confused, and like I'd eaten more butter than popcorn.

Ariana claps her hands like a giddy seal. "Well, you're in luck. Cassie invited Tommy to the wedding. You may even be at the same table since there were more bridesmaids than groomsmen. Now, the fun can really begin."

My stomach turns queasy. Like catching the scent of cheese

in the air like a good little house mouse, I sense something is afoot.

"What?" I ask, but it sounds more like a guttural croak.

Without answering, Ariana whisks into the bathroom. I need one STAT. Forget too much butter, more than a sprinkle of salt tops the proverbial popcorn. Thankfully, I know my way around the resort after working here on and off over the years, and I hurry down the hall to splash some cold water on my face.

Tomaso Costa and I were friends. Best friends. For the duration of my enrollment at college, I did not have a crush on him...at least not that I realized. It wasn't until after I left school, and he was no longer a part of my life, that my feelings appeared like the iceberg and the Titanic.

For ages, after I left school and had the realization, it was like a part of me was missing. I dreamed about meeting him on some lonely road, confessing my feelings, and him replying in kind. Then we'd get married and live happily ever after.

Ha!

Nadine always said my imagination was too vivid. If she'd ever bothered to help Nan and Grampa, she'd have had plenty of time to fantasize about the guy of her dreams.

I wish I could say that I dramatically bump into Tommy right here in the thickly carpeted hallway of the Hawk Ridge Hollow resort, he sweeps me into his arms, asks me to dance, or does any number of other romantic things that are the start of our future. Instead, I careen into one of the catering staff who holds a tray of cupcakes at chest level.

Let's say the two dollops of frosting don't end up in the politest of places.

"Oh, miss, I am so sorry." The young man moves to dab the white and dusty rose frosting with small, matching wafer-like heart sprinkles off the upper part of my copper dress, *ahem*.

I swat his hand away.

"No worries. I got it. Was on my way to the ladies' room

anyway." I dash down the hall, hoping everyone else is in the ballroom and doesn't see my wardrobe malfunction or notice I'm missing. Maybe I can skip the reception altogether. Cassie is having the time of her life. She won't care.

As I round the corner to the elevator, I stop short.

A tall, well-built man wearing a dark blue suit that's tight around his shoulders and biceps, accentuating large muscles, gets out of the elevator.

A mouse-like squeak escapes my lips.

Tommy Costa's brown hair is shorter than in it was college, but his espresso brown eyes are just as thoughtful and just as sharp.

The smirky, half-smile that lifts the corner of his mouth makes me suck in a breath. Like a fine Italian wine, he got better with age. So not fair.

Locked in the tractor beam of Tommy's good looks, I become a Medusa-like statue and not a work of art by Michelangelo or something equally magnificent on display in the hallway at the resort—oh but he is.

Anticipating a gorgeous Italian woman—his wife since things didn't work out after the makeout session with Cassie—to also emerge from the elevator and take his arm, panic flutters and flaps inside, much like my hands, seemingly against my will.

If my legs weren't suddenly encased in cement, granite, or whatever sculptors used during the Renaissance period, refusing to operate, I could probably fly away since my hands won't stop moving. Alternately, I could go back around the corner and run to the stairs at the far end of the hall. My dress is already ruined, it's too late to try not to sweat if I bolt.

But I do perspire. A fine sheen develops at the nape of my neck, above my upper lip, and I shall not mention the situation developing in my armpits.

I know. Ew.

The elevator dings and the door closes, breaking my trance.

No Italian bombshell. It's just Tommy, alone, facing me.

Instinctually, my arms fly in front of my chest as if he'd walked in on me in a dressing room. The remaining frosting sticks to my arms. I start to back away slowly. The only thing that could make this moment more embarrassing, since my body has ceased cooperating with me, is if I were to fall flat on my face.

Instead, the pointy heel of my shoe catches on the carpet, and I windmill backward.

Tommy moves lightning-fast and catches me, falling short of sweeping me into his strong, capable arms—smart to keep me at a distance because of the ill-positioned frosting. Yes, it's still as intact as royal icing on a gingerbread house.

His hands are large and rough, his grip firm and sure. The muscles supporting me are as solid as marble.

My stomach does acrobatics. My cheeks burn like I've been doing the same. This isn't a natural dewy glow. No, it's like I'm in a kitchen with five ovens blazing on a ninety-degree day.

"Merry?" he asks. "What a surprise to see you here."

My eyes must be as big as saucers. "This is not how I imagined this would go."

There he goes with that flirty half-smile again. "You imagined—?"

Against my deepest desire to remain in Tommy's embrace, I wriggle out from his grip and smooth my dress. "No, I meant. Well, I, um..." I temporarily lose myself in those espresso brown eyes.

From a few feet away, someone calls, "Merilee?" I turn to see a stout woman with curly salt and pepper hair. "I didn't know you were working here again? My, the Hawkins' higher-ups are getting mighty creative with their employee uniforms. Is Cece to blame? They couldn't fit me into something like that. You look very fancy. Anyway, I'd love to order a pie from you for Christmas. Cookies I can do, but my specialty doesn't lie in crusts. My sisters each want one too. The pumpkin pie at Thanksgiving was out of this world. Let the season of eating begin. Plus, I'm running the seasonal welcome center on the edge of town. I'm offering cookies, but pies would be a nice addition." She rubs her hands together like she's cooking up an idea.

"Oh, hi, Mrs. Cringle. Thank you." I internally thank her for interrupting the most awkward moment of my life with her chatter.

"Well, don't let me hold you up. Looks like you need to go find an apron, and I'll be in touch about the pie order. Figure on six, no, make that eight."

My smile falters because, at the moment, my non-existent pie baking business is the least of my problems.

Tommy Costa stands so close I'm convinced that my favorite scent is no longer the baking of apples in a buttery crust. No, it's this man's spicy, masculine aftershave. If only it were edible.

Mrs. Cringle disappears around the corner.

"I'm not, I mean I don't, I was a guest at—" My jaw trembles anew under Tommy's gaze as I try to explain that I don't work here. At least not currently. I thumb over my shoulder in the direction of the wedding.

"I know. You were one of Cassie's bridesmaids. I was surprised to see you here after all this time. Figured you'd be in there since I hear they're tossing the bridal bouquet any minute." He looks down and smooths his tie as if stopping himself from saying more.

Is that a reminder that he made out, on my dorm room bed, with the girl who I thought was my good friend? After I thought that maybe, just maybe, we had a little spark? A little special something? Okay, I didn't realize the spark at the time. That was a hindsight thing. A broken heart thing. Not to mention the marriage pact and all the time we spent together, becoming close friends.

The emptiness in my stomach hardens.

"Hawk Ridge Hollow is my hometown. Funny that Cassie decided to say 'I do' here, of all places. I didn't even have to travel." The light little laugh I try for after trying to explain myself sounds more like a piece of metal caught in a window fan.

Tommy quickly glances up and meets my eyes, reminding me that my chest is covered in cupcake frosting. If that weren't the case, or if he weren't him, I might behave like a normal human and ask him something friendly like, *How've you been?*

With splayed fingers, I motion toward the frosting. "I should go take care of this."

"We should catch up," he says at almost the same time.

I nod slowly. "Yeah, sure. Okay." Having forgotten about the issue with my shoe, I jerk forward but catch myself this time.

Tommy is at the ready, but I hold up my hands to indicate I've got this, and because I'm afraid if I dare open my mouth to speak, I might say something ridiculous like, *"Let's ditch this popcorn stand."*

Those were the first corny, dad-joke-esque words he spoke to me at a freshman year orientation event during college. In his defense, the popcorn machine caught on fire and it smelled awful. It became our catchphrase. An inside joke.

"See you inside?" he points toward the ballroom door. "Can't wait to catch up."

And I can hardly catch my breath as I kick off my heels and sprint toward the elevator like a runaway bridesmaid because if I let myself linger, I'll soon be longing for the guy that got away.

CHAPTER 2

TOMMY

Tommy from college and adult Tommy wage an inner battle. The college version of me wants to run after Merry like a puppy dog and not leave her side for the rest of the night. But the adult within that has sense and a modicum of chill tells me to relax, that she needs to freshen up, and she'll be back in no time.

It's been well over ten years since we've seen each other, and she's every bit the same small-town girl with big, beautiful sky-blue eyes that made me believe anything was possible.

Even falling in love. I ignore the twinge in my chest.

It would've been rude to decline Cassie's invitation to her wedding, especially since I live in Hawk Ridge Hollow now. Then again, she was always rude to Merilee, or as I call her Merry. Cassie teased about her name (think lots of singsonging about merrily, merrily, etc.), Cassie regularly ditched her to hang out with people she thought were cooler, and of course, mauling me in the dorm room like a rabid badger—our college mascot was the badger.

I'm surprised the two of them remained friends. After that, I steered clear of Cassie like a case of cooties.

Things between Merry and I were never the same after that incident. Then she got the news about her grandmother's ailing health and left school. I wanted to help, to shield her from pain. I tried to stay in touch, but her replies were sparse. I imagine that was a tough time in her life.

Last I knew, she was in Romania. I knew she was from a small Montana town, but not this one. Okay, I secretly hoped it was this one but didn't want to stalk her like a weirdo.

And maybe I felt a little rejected. But that was stupid college Tommy. Adult Tommy knows better than to be a stubborn nitwit who doesn't know how to communicate. Mostly.

Strange, how we both ended up here. While mingling with the wedding guests, I repeatedly scan the room, seeking the woman with the wavy, buttery blonde hair, sky-blue eyes, adorable round chin, and legs for days.

Maybe she went home to get a change of clothes.

Maybe she's here with her husband.

Maybe she hates me.

It belatedly occurred to my soft-headed college self that what was happening in Merry's dorm room wasn't what it looked like. But I never had a chance to explain.

On mute, my phone repeatedly vibrates in my pocket. Actively retraining myself, because I'm no longer on call, I fight the urge to see who tries to get in touch. The idea is to no longer run on cortisol or adrenalin. To kick back and enjoy myself. I was a first responder—on track to someday becoming a fire captain. On alert, my skin hums, but with focused breathing, I force myself to ease up for now.

After a few songs, during which I politely decline the request to dance from one of Cassie's cousins, I look for Merry.

After the cutting of the giant cupcake wedding cake, the catering staff distributes cupcakes and I keep watch for her.

When the dancing resumes and still no sign of the girl who was my college crush, I finally check my cell.

It's the *Fratelli* thread—Italian for *brothers*. Bruno, Gio, Paulo, Nico, and even Luca light up the text boxes with comments about Ma and Pop. Alarmed, I step outside and immediately call our parents.

After the third ring, my mother picks up. "Marco, dear, I can't figure out the buttons on this thing. Come help me." She speaks in Italian even though she's fluent in English.

"Ma? Ma? It's on. It's me, Tommy. Are you okay?"

"Tomaso? Of course, I'm okay. I just can't seem to figure out how to operate this foolish contraption Giovanni got us. Is it a telephone? A camera? A meteorologist? Why can't it pick one thing?"

In the background, my father says, "I've always told you, never trust a man who says he can do anything. Yeah, he can do anything, alright, like take your money, then slap you upside the head with your own wallet."

I press my hand to my forehead. "You guys are alright though?"

"Yes, of course. We're fine. Just got back from a lovely dinner with the Patels. Did you know their daughter runs their restaurant now?"

"No, Ma. I didn't know that because I don't know who the Patels are."

"Well, if you'd come home once in a while, I could introduce you. Padma is single," my mother chimes in her Italian accent.

"I was home three weeks ago, and I thought you wanted me to find a nice Italian girl."

"Italian, Indian, American. I don't care anymore. Just find someone."

"That's getting straight to the point," I mutter as I start to relax, knowing they're not in imminent danger.

Again, from the background, my father says, "I've always told you never to trust a man who can't find a good woman."

Merry comes to mind, dressed in that copper gown that

accentuated her hourglass figure. My pulse picks up again but for an entirely new reason this time. "That's a new one, Pop."

"No, it's an oldie but goodie," he hollers.

"This thing is so loud," my mother shouts.

"You probably have it on the speaker function since Dad can hear me."

"Yes, right. I'm speaking to you," she says as if she's talking to a dullard.

I shake my head, not bothering to explain. Bruno signed them up for a seniors' technology class after Giovanni introduced the cellphone, but I doubt they attended.

"Listen, this thing has been beeping off the hook. We've had calls from the credit card company, the bank, the IRS, and even a Liegerian prince. He calls every week—"

I cut her off. "Tell me you didn't share any of your personal information."

"Of course not, but Tomaso, I'm not going to let some blood-thirsty pirates hold a prince captive," Ma says.

"I've always said that there's no escaping death and taxes," Dad adds.

I scrub my hand down my face. "You gave the callers money?"

"Just a few wires. Like I used to do for Nonna after I left Genoa."

I let out a long puff of breath. My parents fell prey to phone scammers. This is bad. "Ma, Pop, pack your bags. You're coming to Hawk Ridge Hollow. Oh, and don't answer your phone unless it's a call from a Costa."

If they protest, I don't hear because I hang up and return to the Fratelli text thread to call an emergency meeting.

Afterward, I take one more loop through the ballroom, searching for Merry. No luck. Perhaps we'll run into each other in town. Had I not learned that my parents were just scammed, possibly repeatedly, I'd ask her to dance, catch up, and try to patch things up because I'm not too stupid to realize that what she saw happening with Cassie back in college threw off our friendship, our budding relationship...a potential future.

But she never gave me a chance to explain.

After blasting out a bunch of texts in reply to my brothers, I return to my empty house, dig out the cards, and set up the table. While waiting, I put my mind to figuring out a solution that preserves my parents' dignity as independent adults but also moves them closer so I can make sure they don't send money to a Liegerian prince.

I roll my eyes and pray.

A few months ago, Dallen Hawkins alerted me to a real estate opportunity that I couldn't pass up. Having retired from the fire department, I had the flexibility to invest, especially since it meant I'd be closer to my sister Frankie, her husband Rusty, and their growing family.

Granted, it gets cold up here in the winter, but I have the space for Ma and Pop. Plus, it would save them money and they could rent out their apartment in New York City.

About six months ago, I went through their bills with them and automated most everything, then created a budget. They've always been responsible citizens that contribute to their church and community, but lately, they've gotten lax, a little forgetful. As the oldest brother, it's my duty to make sure they're taken care of. Their finances weren't dire, but not as robust as I'd like, especially since they make an annual return trip to Italy for a month during the summer.

As I skim the online banking app, wire transfers amounting to thousands of dollars shout at me in big, bold red numbers.

I'm such a dummy and immediately set up alerts so I know about these kinds of things in the future.

Tension builds across my shoulders. We have to do something and do it fast.

Luca lives nearby. I think Gio is in town shooting for a

skiwear brand, and Nico isn't far. But it might be a while before Bruno and Paulo show up from the city. Thing is, when one of us calls a meeting, we drop everything. That's family. Those are the unspoken rules. As per tradition, we break the ice with a game of cards.

Footsteps stomp across my front porch and I wonder which of my brothers got here first. In our order of play, they sit to the right of the card dealer, me, meaning they go first.

Instead, Frankie appears in the doorway with her hands on her hips. "I heard you called an emergency meeting." My sister's tone is sharp.

"Who's the traitor? Who told you?" My eyes narrow.

"Oh, stop. You guys have always been overly protective of me. I can handle whatever is going on with Ma and Pop." She waddles over and plops down.

"You're nine months pregnant with your fourth child," I say, pointing out the obvious because I don't want to cause her undue stress.

"And I'm as strong as an ox. Ma had seven of us. I can handle news about our parents. Seriously, I got this."

I lean my elbows on the card table. "I know you do. It's just that you have a family now. The rest of us are unattached. We didn't want to burden you."

"Our parents are not a burden. What's the diagnosis?" she asks, voice suddenly soft.

I straighten. "They're not sick."

She frowns. "Oh, then what's the problem?"

I explain the phone call scams and show her the damage on the banking app.

"I'd like to blame a language barrier, but Ma and Pop are good at English. That's not it. They're just—"

I finish for her. "Retired. In relaxation mode. Possibly vulnerable to scammers pulling on their heartstrings."

Frankie tosses me a pointed look. Look up the word *relaxed* in the dictionary, and you won't find my photo there. I'm afraid that it's gotten worse since I left my job.

"...And susceptible to being taken advantage of. What are we going to do?" she asks.

Frankie and I brainstorm as the cast of characters who've been a constant in my life slowly appear, starting with Luca who lives at the foot of the mountains in the old family cabin which he recently renovated and expanded. It's what brought Frankie here in the first place.

"Luca, are you and Rusty in a secret beard-growing contest?" Frankie asks.

"Some women like the rugged look," he says in his low growl.

"And brutish cavemen terrify most women," she retorts.

"You married Rusty."

She wears a rare smile. "He's an exception."

Headlights beam across the front window and Nico, the youngest, appears. "What have I missed?"

"I'm developing a plan." That's not true. So far, I've got nothing other than demanding our parents move in with me. Never mind kicking and screaming, they'll go for the throat. How can we convince them it's a good idea?

Nico flashes me a dubious look, not because he knows I'm full of it, but because, all too often, my plans involve him having to step outside his comfort zone. We don't talk much about his love life, but it's safe to say that he isn't a Casanova like Gio.

"Who's missing? Bruno—?"

"He's going to make you call him Bryan," Frankie says. "And he texted, saying he'll have to video chat in."

Ah, so he's the traitor, meaning he told our sister about the secret meeting. The two of them must conspire on the side. Noted.

My brow furrows. "That leaves Paulo and Gio."

Just then the *chuff, chuff, chuff* of a helicopter's blades comes from outside. We all wait, not surprised by our jet-setting brother's grand entrance. Or in this case, chopper-setting.

Giovanni enters on a gust of chilly air. He hugs Frankie like she's fragile and gives us a lazy salute before kicking his boots up on the table.

I lift one eyebrow in warning, and he drops them.

"Where's Paulo?" Gio asks.

"*Non comunicativo*," Nico says.

"I'll fill in for him," Frankie says while getting Bruno on the video chat and setting her phone up at the table as if he were sitting here with us. She fills Paulo's chair and also relays to our brothers everything I told her about Ma and Pop.

I shuffle then deal the cards, preparing to tell the story that's become our custom when calling a family meeting. Incidentally, the last time we did this was when we found out Frankie had fallen in love with the enemy—a long-standing family feud between the Costas and Hawkins clan that has since been resolved.

"Our grandfather's parents wanted him to marry a woman in Italy. She was from a good family and a lovely girl. Francesco Costa liked her but didn't want to be hemmed in."

So far, the six of us boys follow in his footsteps. All single.

I continue, "Francesco was young. So he told his parents that he was going to travel for a month. That turned into a year, which turned into more. But he grew up during that time and decided he knew what he wanted. He found himself in Hawk Ridge Hollow. The coldest place on earth, according to him."

"It's not so bad," Luca interrupts. "I can't say I'm mad that he won the cabin in a bet with Charles Hawkins."

"Glad we're neighbors," Frankie says. She moved from the cottage next door to Rusty's house after they got married, leaving the old family cabin available.

To move things along, Gio waves his hand. "We know the rest of the story. Our Aunt Elena showed up to bring Nanno home. She fell in love with Charlie Hawkins, but no one was good enough for his sister." He cuts a glance at Frankie.

Once upon a time, we forbid our sister to get married to Rusty Hawkins.

"I happen to know you and Rusty have Wordle competitions all the time," I say, referring to the fact that we were all dubious about our sister's relationship with the former hockey star in the beginning but quickly absorbed Rusty Hawkins into the Costa clan.

Nico picks up the story. "The friendship between our *nanno* and Charlie fell apart. That started the feud. Zia Elana really liked Charlie, but she agreed to let him go if Francesco returned to Italy with her. And he did. He married *Nonna*. Had he not, we wouldn't be here."

"And she wouldn't have taught me how to cook." Frankie smiles fondly.

"So what would our grandfather have done if in this predicament?" I ask per custom.

"I thought you said you have a plan," Nico says.

"It's a formality, little bro," Bruno says through the speaker. "Bottom line, we're not sending Ma and Pop to a care home."

We all balk.

"No way. I'm taking them in. If for some reason, I couldn't do it, there are six of you," I say to make the point clear.

"Paulo isn't here," Luca adds.

"Paulo would do anything for them."

"But not for us," Nico mutters.

He's been scarce for the last six months.

"I'm hungry. Do you have anything to eat?" Frankie starts to get to her feet.

Gio launches out of his chair and paws through my kitchen cabinets, searching for something for our pregnant sister to snack on.

I snap my fingers as inspiration bubbles into my mind like

cheese on a pizza. "Cooking. We'll open a restaurant like our grandparents did."

"Tommy, as you so kindly pointed out earlier, I'm nine months pregnant. This baby is coming by Christmas whether I like it or not. No way can I open a new restaurant right now."

I shake my head, feeling overwhelmed with warmth that my siblings are here and with confidence that together, we can do anything. "You can be the consultant, Frankie."

Bruno moans because she tends to micromanage us. Then again, she has children she can torment now.

"We'll open a pizza parlor." The ideas come to me hot and fast.

"And how will opening a pizza shop help our parents?" Luca asks.

"They'll be our top employees," I answer.

Gio squints. "They retired."

"They'll work there in name only. We'll run the place. It'll be a family business, giving them an excuse to come out here. I'll convince them to stay, set them up nicely, and not have to worry about them wiring money to a Liegerian prince."

"Is Liegeria an actual country?" Nico asks.

Gio chuckles. "Definitely not."

"I'll run the place. Boots on the ground. Frankie, you can create the menu. Bruno, you'll be our numbers guy and keep the books. Gio, you can do PR to get the word out."

"I have the farm," Luca says, bowing out.

"And you'll do inventory at night," I add, pointing at him.

"What about Paulo?" Frankie asks.

"I'll talk to him." If he'd ever answer his phone.

"And me?" Nico asks.

"Uh, you can be the delivery boy, bus boy, box folding boy..."

My baby brother glares at me.

I brush my hands together, problem solved.

"You do realize we all have careers and lives?" Bruno says through the phone.

"Yes, but except for Frankie, none of us have families."

"Not yet," Nico says.

Gio, who has been engaged so many times we've lost count, grunts.

"Right, but if we're supporting our parents, what about us? How are we supposed to survive?" Bruno asks.

"Tips," I say.

"I'm not that cute," Nico says.

"I am," Gio counters with a smolder.

"I'm out. As I said, I have the farm," Luca says.

"The Christmas tree farm? That's a part-time gig," I remind him.

Luca shifts uncomfortably at the mention of Christmas.

"Say it," Frankie taunts, eyes mischievous.

He refuses to use the word *Christmas*. I say give the guy a break. Frankie employs tough love.

"Grinch. Grump. Scrooge." She glowers, trying to get a rise out of him.

Before they break down in sibling war chaos, I whistle. "Listen, you'll all get paid. Don't worry. But we're going to give at least ten percent to Ma and Pop. Think about it this way, they supported our ungrateful keisters for eighteen years. Each. Can any of you imagine having seven kids?"

The question ought to silence us brothers with introspection. Instead, I sense a twitchy fear in the room. Ma and Pop would do anything to find us each in the family way. Looking at it objectively, I know they love us, but also imagine they want us each to have a fleet of caring offspring to take care of us should we make donations to a "Free the Liegerian Prince" fund.

"It wasn't just financially that they helped us either," I add. "They've been amazing parents. We can do this. We have to. We owe them. But they can't know." I stab the air with my pointer finger.

"What if they see money filtering into their account?" Bruno asks from the screen on the table.

"They won't. They didn't notice it filtering out," I say. I hope.

"Some of us have important jobs that we can't just leave," Bruno says.

I roll my eyes. "Nothing is more important than family."

His silence confirms that he knows I'm right.

"If memory serves, you are not to be trusted in the kitchen," Luca says.

Wincing, I deal the cards. "Remember, I'm a firefighter. I can handle a little heat."

They look at me as if they're not so sure, but no one suggests an alternative, so it's as good as a done deal.

"There's a vacant shop on Main Street in town—" Luca says then abruptly cuts himself off as if regretting sharing the information.

"Excellent. I'll look into it first thing tomorrow morning. Gio, please arrange for Ma and Pop to travel here. Bruno, pack up the apartment. I have plenty of room for them. Frankie, when they get here, please distract them with your adorable children. Luca, don't scare anyone away."

"What about me?" Nico asks.

"Come up with a name."

"Pizza Parlor, Pizza Palace, Pizza Pie, Pizza Villa..." he starts.

"Pizza Boy," Luca says around a chuckle.

"Frankie's Five Brothers," Bruno adds.

"But there are six of us," Nico says then scowls as if he knows he's the one Bruno left out.

"Ignore him. Plus, Paulo's not here," Frankie says. "How about Maria and Marco's Pizza, after Ma and Pop?"

"Has a good ring to it, but Pop will probably have some chestnut he claims he 'always says' about naming things after them and it being bad luck or something," I say.

"For now, let's call it Hawk Ridge Hollow Pizza."

We all agree with varying nods of assent.

Everyone disperses, leaving me with my thoughts.

There are more details to opening a dining establishment than I care to think about at this late hour, but our parents came from the old country and made it here in America. They taught us to work hard to achieve our goals and that anything is possible.

My mind repeatedly lands on Merilee Ketchum, blonde, beautiful, and back in Hawk Ridge Hollow. Officially, we were only ever friends, but she didn't really date in college. We had some fun times for sure. A few crazy ones too.

I pull out a box that I haven't opened since college and riffle through sports memorabilia, flyers from campus events, some random junk, and lots of photos. Tucked in the stack is a folded piece of paper. I unfold it and read:

I, Merilee Merry Ketchum, do hereby promise to marry Tomaso Marco Costa if, by the time we both reach the age of thirty, we are still single. Upon entering into holy matrimony we will follow up with a popcorn-themed reception.

I wrote the same thing below and we both signed and dated it. Then we amended it to add these rules:

- Passenger gets to control the radio
- No secrets allowed
- No burping or farting
- Don't share toothbrushes
- Always be honest
- Plan one date per month
- Above all, trust each other
- Arguments resolved with an offering of popcorn

- Put the toilet seat down

I chuckle to myself because, at the time, we thought thirty was old. That's funny because it feels like we only wrote this yesterday. The big three-oh has come and gone, yet I forgot about this pact. I'm now thirty-six and single.

Likely, Merilee Merry Ketchum is happily married. She may even have kids. I should ask Frankie if she knows her.

No, I should focus on bailing out our parents. I tuck the marriage pact into a spiral notebook I also find in the box and open to a new page to begin outlining the business plan for the pizza shop.

I try to put Merry and the marriage pact out of my mind. I try and fail. However, I can't afford to fail my mother and father.

Although, I can't help but think I already somehow failed my college best friend.

CHAPTER 3

MERILEE

Even though I'd like to have returned to Cassie's wedding with my head held high and my dignity intact, there was no rescuing the satin gown from the frosting stain. After removing the offending confection, I returned to the bridal suite to see if there were any spare wedding-appropriate garments for me.

I spotted Nan's handkerchief, my gift to Cassie, discarded on the table. My heart sank because I'm not sure Cassie and I have the same definition of friendship. In fact, I overheard her and Ariana talking about how I'm hopelessly single. Then Cassie said, "*More like helplessly.*"

Back home in my kitchen, as I roll out pie dough, I try to let the comment go. Yes, it's almost nine pm, but it's never too late to bake.

Nadine calls this stress baking. I call it delicious.

Plus, I didn't even get a cupcake out of the wedding day deal. Instead, I have a ruined dress to add to my collection of thirteen bridesmaid's gowns. A baker's dozen. That might be a record. Perhaps I could make myself a quilt or stitch together a wedding dress of my own.

I can't upset the ratio of salt to fat in my dough, so I don't let these emotions drip-drop into the bowl in the form of tears.

Nan would dab my eyes with the handkerchief because she was a practical woman—not the kind of person to have a sitting room for guests only or let an empty plastic bag go to waste. Yet, that handkerchief was special—unused. It's not like my grandfather blew his nose in it or anything. Why didn't Cassie care?

A sigh escapes as I think about Nan. I'd like to say I miss her, and in many ways I do. Although she's no longer here and is now in heaven, she's not lost. I feel like she's always with me, especially when I make pies.

This time it's apple with a bit of the cheddar goat cheese blend I got from Farmer Eddleston. I'm determined to win Captain Hoof over with appreciation for the milk products provided by his lady goats.

The next morning, the wind whips against the window shutters as I wake from a dream about Nan. She insisted I open a pizza place, but I think my subconscious' wires crossed and she meant a pie place—a bakery.

I'm currently unemployed after being laid off from the catering company where I'd hoped to become the lead baker. The owner moved south after deciding the Hawk Ridge Hollow's winters weren't for her. I considered following but didn't want to miss Christmas here. It truly is the most wonderful place to be during the most wonderful time of the year despite the frigid temperatures and frequent storms.

There was also the issue of not wanting to dip into my savings. See, I pretend it's not there so I can someday open the pie shop, but that leaves me relatively broke.

This would be a good time to receive an unexpected inheritance (minus someone else dying), win the lottery (if only I played), or have an unexpected windfall (the only wind is out of the northeast, and boy howdy, is it blowing). I also wouldn't say no to finding a treasure in the backyard. That wouldn't be bad. As long as it isn't cursed.

Short of that and with the letter to Santa still on the table, meaning no relationship prospects, I do have this dream of mine. A flash of excitement rushes through me like a hummingbird when, for the first time, it realizes that it can fly.

Feeling inspired, I pull out my business plan and review it, wondering if I could start small, right here in my kitchen baking holiday pies for people like Mrs. Cringle and her sisters, along with selling some at the seasonal welcome center on the edge of town. Maybe entice a few others over the holidays and grow from there.

But what would I call it?

I repeatedly come back to that issue, stopping me from moving forward. Only one name comes to mind and his initials are *TC*.

I do my best thinking in the shower and nearly convince myself to go for it, name or not. First, I want to make sure Mrs. Cringle actually wants the pies and wasn't just being polite. She runs the toy and craft store a few doors down from Mom & Lollipop's candy shop.

On my way there, the obvious name floats into my head. I could call my pie shop Hawk Ridge Hollow Pies. It doesn't quite have a ring to it, but it is straight to the point.

As I pass through town, clouds cover the tops of the mountains. It's almost December and Christmas lights and decorations start to appear, at odds with the gloomy day. The wind whips furiously, scattering the few leaves still on the ground across the road and onto my car. They catch in the windshield wipers, and I flip them on. A piece of paper, also dusted up in the gust, flattens against my windshield. It stops the wipers, so I pull over.

My hair blows in every direction as I peel the paper off the glass. It says, *For Rent* and has a telephone number underneath. The flurry of wind catches my scarf and the piece of paper, carrying them both away. I go chasing after them when a car honks.

Cassie rolls down the window. "Hey, be careful." She squints. "Oh, it's you. Hi, Merilee."

I wave limply, having hoped I could avoid seeing her since I scooted out early last night.

"Heard you had a close encounter with a cupcake." She titters.

And Tommy, but best not to think about him right now.

"We're leaving for our honeymoon. Goodbye wind and cold, hello beach. Cancun here we come!" Cassie hoots.

"Babe, you know I love skiing and you promised we could come back," Leon whines from the driver's seat.

Cassie grumbles. "We'll see about that. You know I always get my way." She laughs again.

I vaguely recall the marriage pact Tommy and I made, including our rules to keep things fair—while acknowledging the natural give and take of a healthy relationship. I wonder if he remembers.

My stomach dips. I hope not. Mostly.

"*Bon voyage. Adios.* Or is it *ciao*? Anyway, *ta ta* and good luck. Get me out of this boring town," Cassie says as they peel away.

"More like good riddance," I mumble as the wind seems to thrust them down the street, taking my scarf with it. It whirls and dances in the air as I make chase.

I rescue my scarf from the stoop of the only vacant shop on Main Street. The torn awning flaps in the wind. Flakes of paint peel off the doorframe. The window is cracked and dusty. It's Hawk Ridge Hollow's lone eyesore on an otherwise cheerful and bustling street populated with quaint shops, amazing restaurants, trees, park benches, and plaster statues of hawks that are about a yard tall and painted by local organizations like the Boy Scouts, Friends of the Library, and others. The Velvet Curtain Theater and Arts Center painted the one by my car. It wears a black top hat and scarf. I get snowman-inspired vibes.

Just as I'm about to go back to my car, I notice that the handmade sign on the door to the vacant storefront matches the one in my hand *For Rent*.

I peer inside and see the outline of tables hidden under dust cloths and a massive woodfire oven on the far wall. The faded lettering etched on the glass P-I-Z-Z-A, reminds me this was a pizza place when I was little. It's sat empty all these years. My dream with Nan, urging me to open a pizza place, comes to mind and I chuckle at the humor.

I peer inside again. The till sits on the counter, there are several display cases, and an ample dining room.

My body does a tiny jolt as a light bulb goes off inside, illuminating an idea.

Could I rent this place out, fix it up, and open a bakery?

The answer doesn't come to me from my inner voice shouting a loud *YES!*. Rather, it's Mrs. Cringle approaching from down the sidewalk and calling, "Yoo-hoo! Merilee!"

I wave back and tighten my scarf around my neck.

Despite the weather, she's as cheerful as ever. "Sure is blustery. Fancy meeting you again. I was just on my way to pay a visit to Martha at the Hawk Post—we have to plan our route through the Christmas market next month."

I should apply for a stall, but it's probably too late. I heard they book out six months in advance, which is par for the course here in Hawk Ridge Hollow. "I was heading over to your shop to bring you a pie."

"I haven't placed my order yet."

"This is a sample. I made a list of options for you and your sisters."

"You are so sweet. I'll take one of each, but I'm wondering if you'd be up for a Christmas barter. I had one of my usual artisans bow out of the church Christmas bazaar. How about you set up a table. I'll waive the entry feet." She winks. "And you still bake my sisters and me the pies. The girls will pay you, of course." Her smile is as warm as ever.

While the Christmas Market lasts for the duration of December, the Christmas Bazaar is for one weekend only. However, both are hard to get into as a vendor. It's a start. Perhaps this year I could have a table, next year a stall at the market, then graduate to a shop. Baby steps.

"That's generous. I can't say no."

We stand there for a few more moments chatting about details. She glances at the paper in my hand. "Please tell me you're thinking of renting this old place and opening a bakery."

"We already have the Beanery in town," I say, suddenly self-conscious and feeling out of my depth. That's an ocean-size prospect and I'm still treading water in the kiddie pool.

Mrs. Cringle pats her tummy. "There is no such thing as too many baked goods. Tobias Marley owns the former pizza parlor. Don't let him drive too hard a bargain. I imagine he's losing money with it sitting here vacant all this time."

"Tobias Marley," I repeat, trying to place the somewhat familiar name.

"He and his wife ran the Hawk Ridge Hollow Sweetheart contest. If I recall, you won one year, didn't you?"

My cheeks warm as the memory of wearing the sash and riding in the July Fourth parade comes back. "It was so sad about Mrs. Marley's passing."

"Tobias has never been the same." Mrs. Cringle glances at the empty shop. "Go on, pretend I'm Cecilia, giving you a little nudge." She makes a chicken wing with her elbow.

"Do you mean Nan?"

"Yep. She always dreamed of opening a bakery but gave her pies away for free."

I nod slowly, recalling how generous she was and knowing the reason she didn't pursue a pie shop was that she unexpectedly had two little girls to look after.

Mrs. Cringle points to the phone number on the sign. "Go on. I'll wait here for moral support."

My heart beats like I'm swimming laps. Taking a deep breath, I dial the number. A gruff-sounding man answers, and we set up an appointment for ten am. That's in half an hour.

"And that's how it's done. Now, if you can get it open by Christmas, I bet you'll have more than my pies to bake." Mrs. Cringle holds out her hands for the one I hold.

After we say goodbye, I get back in the car and stare at the vacant shop as panic and a twinge of excitement bounce off each other inside of me.

I'm a small-town girl who always wanted to get out of the small town until Nan passed away. I tried numerous times but always find myself back here. Lately, I've wanted to put down roots and have a business and family of my own.

But one thing at a time.

I shouldn't think about relationships. I'm no hot prospect especially not after the frosting fiasco at the wedding, Tommy probably told Cassie. I bet they had a good laugh. I know it's dumb to let one incident back in college throw me off my game —not that I ever had any game when it came to guys. Nadine also calls me "Garlic bread, the original man-repellant." Anyway, the whole thing with Cassie cut into my confidence in a way that I can't seem to shake.

I bet she'd come up with a jab relating me to shake cheese— the parmesan kind on tables at most pizza places.

Plus, for a second there, I thought Tommy was *the one*. Even though I haven't really had a robust dating life since we parted ways, I've never felt the same flutter, kick, or whoosh inside that I did for him when around other men.

Too bad I realized this after it was too late.

Take last night for example. No, never mind. I don't want to think about that because there's no way Tommy would be interested in me, especially after how I successfully managed to embarrass myself front and back, top to bottom, inside and out.

Maybe the Nadines and Cassies of the world are right. Nothing is interesting about me. I'm a cookie-cutter person, leading a cookie-cutter life. Not that I have anything against cookies. Don't get me wrong, I love them. But I'm more of a pie girl.

Nan's voice *tsks* in my mind. She'd scold me for these thoughts. Mrs. Cringle too, no doubt. But I don't have evidence to prove otherwise. My grandmother taught me a lot of traditional skills. Quilting, baking, preserving. Heck, I can milk a cow, but that doesn't prove very lucrative in the present economy or in the dating world.

Just imagine what my dating app profile would look like with those credentials:

Hi! I'm Merilee Ketchum, a woman who loves gardening, cross-stitching, and reading. I'd be the perfect companion to bore you out of your mind. But don't worry, I'm useful too. I know how to sew, bake bread, and keep chickens. Not to mention I can operate a hunting rifle. Also, I'm a college dropout, am better at giving than receiving, hence my spotty work record, and am looking for someone who likes pie.

Then again, here I am, still living in this small town where it isn't unusual for people to ride along Main Street on horseback or for families to go door to door for Christmas caroling.

Over the years, I've had glimpses of city living, but I feel an emptiness when there, a pull back home. I thought I had to be worldly and adventurous, striking out on my own. But I like seeing familiar faces every day, knowing where to get a cup of milk if I'm out, and that Mac Eddleston's goats don't actually mean any harm. Okay, Captain Hoof with the really twisty and pointy horns definitely has it in for me, but I believe we can work that out if given time and an opportunity to build a trusting relationship.

Even though my heart is cut in two—half longing for love and half pursuing my pie-in-the-sky dream—I resolve to do what I can with what I have. That was another one of Nan's sayings.

I glance up at the empty storefront. I can do this.

Pie shop, here I come.

I hope.

I go across the street to the Beanery and grab a cup of cocoa to prepare for the meeting with Tobias Marley. When I return at two minutes to ten, a tall figure with broad shoulders stands by the door to the vacant shop. Mr. Marley is a vague memory from my teenage years, but I distinctly recall that he was rather squat. Even when not in my Hawk Ridge Hollow Sweetheart heels, I towered over him.

Even though the air is now still, a shiver brushes through me.

The man in front of the shop is unmistakably Tommy Costa. I consider dodging behind a nearby tree to hide, but a worker wraps Christmas lights around the trunk.

"Merry," Tommy calls with a wave.

My pulse jitters. "Oh, hi. It's like déjà vu."

His eyebrow lifts in question.

"I just ran into Mrs. Cringle again and now you. The same as last night but in reverse." My words take on a nervous chatter, kind of like my teeth. I tell myself it's because of the air temperature.

His lips press together with concern. "About that, where'd you go?"

"Oh, the dress was ruined and—"

Before I finish my sentence an Oldsmobile covered in dirt and road salt backfires with a *kaboom* as it pulls into the spot in front of the empty pizza shop.

Tommy and I both spin in that direction as a man with a sizeable paunch gets out of the vehicle. As he approaches us, he sneers at the worker putting up the Christmas lights.

Please don't be Tobias Marley.

As he gets closer, the man with sparse dark hair comes into focus. He used to have a friendly smile, bushy eyebrows, and love in his eyes for Mrs. Marley, the original Hawk Ridge Hollow Sweetheart. Grief at losing her seems to have done him in, except for the eyebrows. They're as thick as ever.

Mr. Marley stands opposite us on the sidewalk and says, "Today is my lucky day. You must be Merilee and Tommy, I take it?" His tone is flat like fortune is not on his side.

We both nod and exchange a questioning look.

He peers at me more closely. "I remember you. Must've been over ten years ago or more by now. You won the Hawk Ridge Hollow Sweetheart contest. Most girls who achieve the honor go on to bigger, better things." He glances at my hands.

Clasped in front of me, they're half in prayer that this encounter veers in a more promising direction than this rough start and half hiding my ringless finger because all the previous Hawk Ridge Hollow Sweethearts had suitors banging down their doors.

Mr. Marley continues, "And usually they get snatched up and married before the Hawk Ridge Hollow parade and founding day festivities are over."

My smile falters at the reminder that I'm single. If only Tommy liked string cheese and garlic bread. Then again, he's Italian. Although, if the scene with Cassie was any indication, he prefers girls with a little more style, who can readily make pop-culture references, and prefer city life.

Tommy lifts an eyebrow in my direction because I never mentioned the local contest—mostly because Nadine was so mad that I won, it was easier to pretend it didn't happen. She decided it would be funny to play hide and seek with my crown and sash the morning of the parade. Have I mentioned she's my older sister?

I vaguely recall the marriage pact with Tommy and how there was a *no secrets* clause.

Mr. Marley pulls out a set of keys and fits one in the lock. "Let's go inside and get away from this miserable wind."

I can't tell if the whirling in my stomach is excitement or nervousness.

Tommy flashes a smile, and I decide that it's both.

CHAPTER 4

TOMMY

Merry coughs when Mr. Marley pulls a cloth off a table. The dust motes dance in the air like snowflakes—or the popcorn explosion that was our original meet-cute. If it were just her and me, the moment would be poetic or laugh-worthy. We were the kind of friends that appreciated both.

Mr. Marley drops heavily into a chair that creaks under his girth.

"This place has good bones, despite the dust. Lots of potential." Sadness tugs at the corners of his mouth.

Merry and I join him at the table. Our elbows bump, sending a little thrill through me despite our thick jackets. Gosh, I miss her smile, laughing together, and the closeness that developed between us over time.

I can't help but think about how this sudden turn of events with my family enterprise is only made more unusual with her here. We're both quiet as if deep in thought, or shock. Not sure which.

"Okay, ladies first. Tell me why you want to rent this place." Tobias Marley reviews a piece of paper.

Oh. I see. It's a joint interview. We're both interested in the space. Competing for it. How inconvenient.

Merry points at herself. "Okay. Thank you for this opportunity, sir. I want to rent this space and open a pie shop."

"Why?" His eyes narrow like a timer ticks down, pressuring her to come up with a quick answer.

Wearing a sweet smile, she says, "My best memories were baking pies with my grandmother."

"Cecilia Ketchum, if I recall. Good woman." Mr. Marley nods as if recollecting the past.

Late one spring night back at school, while we watched for shooting stars, I recall Merry mentioning that being in the kitchen with her Nan was her happy place, where she felt most loved and appreciated.

Being with Merry is mine. She's always made for great company, but she also made me laugh, think, and feel—even though my thick-headed college self didn't exactly recognize it at the time.

After the accident that not too long ago landed me in the hospital with irreparable lung damage, I left the fire department only to enter a cave of depression. Who was I without my brothers in the company, without a purpose? Thankfully, I mostly emerged from despair, but being with Merry again makes me confidently believe I'll never return to that dark place. Like I'm free and anything is possible.

Her voice floats to me like the scent of something yummy from the oven. "I bake pies for family and friends, events occasionally. Everyone always tells me I should go into business. I've worked at various jobs around town, including the resort, and am looking for something new. Something of my own."

Marley grunts as if her elevator pitch didn't quite sell him on the idea.

"And I have an entire business plan." She sets a binder with colored tabs on the table as if prepared to present her case.

The spiral notebook I brought with a sketch of my ideas for a pizza place suddenly seems paltry in comparison.

As if he's already passed on her proposal, Marley doesn't look at it. He points at me. "Your turn."

I clear my throat, completely unprepared for this unconventional interview. If this is an elevator pitch, the cables just snapped and I'm plunging to the lobby. "My name is Tommy Costa, sir. I recently retired from the fire department in New York City. My sister married Rusty Hawkins, and I relocated to the area to be closer to family." I leave off the part about the lung damage and how much I miss my fire family.

"I'm less interested in who you are than why you're here. The question was, why do you want to rent this space?" Mr. Marley crosses his arms in front of his chest and leans back.

I answer, "I'd like to open a pizza place. Well, my five brothers and I would."

He tips his head from side to side as if considering my response. "Fitting, considering its previous use for the same. If it's going to be a family affair, why aren't they here with you? Don't they want to see it?"

I wince. "Sir, there are five of them."

He grunts. "You mentioned. Could get crowded in the kitchen."

I go on to explain how we'd divvy up the jobs.

He smacks his lips together as if he sees right through me to how flimsy my plan is. Well-intentioned, but about as solid as the discolored doily crumpled up on the side of the table. "So they'd be more like your employees."

"I may be the oldest, but I'm not dumb enough to tell them that," I joke then chuckle to lighten the mood.

Marley leans back, unamused. "Do either of you have business experience?"

Merry and I look at each other as if we'll find the answer

there. Regretfully, I have no idea what she's been doing with her life all these years.

"Well, no..." she starts, shivering a little. It is drafty in here. Nothing a woodfired pizza oven wouldn't fix.

My spine lengthens with pride. "Served the fire department for over twelve years then—"

"But you've never run a restaurant or operated a service industry-based enterprise?" Mr. Marley asks.

"No," we both answer at the same time as if we're applying to rent the place together.

"I have to admit, that's not promising." Marley's gaze travels from mine to Merry's and back again. "I don't feel confident renting the space to you individually. Too much liability. You need a business partner. Pizza and pie or whatever."

We both start to protest at how that's not possible.

"Hold on. Let me finish. I propose you go in together." Marley claps his hands and holds them there as if to make his point.

"Propose?" I stutter, recalling the old marriage pact I found last night.

"But I'd be making pies," Merry says, clearly not having the same memory, and remaining in the present moment.

"And I'd be selling pizza." Does he want me to share the pizza place with a pie baker? That's not going to happen. As a former fireman, I'm all about teamwork, but I'm not sharing the dough.

"Pizza, pie? Is there really a difference?" Marley asks.

"Yes," we reply in unison.

"Go into business together. Two heads are better than one. Also, if one of you quits or goes under, the other one will be able to keep the lights on, if you know what I mean."

I glance at Merry and pump my hands, wanting to slow things down and have a conversation about this. "Sir, with all due respect—"

"That's my best and final offer. Take it or leave it. I've had interest from CoffeeHut, the national chain. Signori Pepperoni, the popular pizza place in the city with several locations and growing their franchises, has also solicited me for use of the space. I've been in Hawk Ridge Hollow for a long time and know the townspeople would pitch a fit if I lease the spot to a corporation, not to mention my wife would roll over in her grave if she saw me rent out her family's shop to that kind of business. But I have to make a dollar too...and the property taxes have caught up with me," he adds darkly.

"So you're suggesting we open a pizza and pie shop together at the same time in the same place?" I ask to clarify, not quite trusting that I understood.

"You got it. And to sweeten the deal, you have until Christmas to begin operations, otherwise, I'll get the big boys in here. I don't want anything coming between me and the rent check if you catch my meaning. Coffee Hut and Signori Pepperoni are good for it. But I'll give you a chance to prove yourselves. That you're the best business for the spot."

"I'd have to think about it," Merry says hesitantly.

On the other side of the window, an older couple walks slowly past and then pauses to watch as a worker hangs a wreath on the lantern post. They smile, reminding me of my parents.

"I'm ready to start now," I declare without thinking as if the timer has nearly run out.

Merry glances at me as if overwhelmed. "It's just that—"

"Then we don't have a deal." Marley starts toward the door. "It's all or nothing."

I scratch my chin. "Can you legally do this?"

"My place, my rules. Take it or leave it."

My jaw is set. Up against the clock, Merry's jaw trembles as if her thoughts struggle to translate to words under pressure. I can't imagine she'd want to go into business with a pizza maker if her specialty is pie, especially since she has a business plan. I also don't want to lose this opportunity.

Marley's hand closes around the door knob.

I have to do something to help my parents and don't want to return to my siblings with my tail between my legs. Commercial properties are at a premium in Hawk Ridge Hollow. The only other option, after my extensive research this morning, would be to build a new location farther out from the downtown area. There isn't time for that and if we were to pool our resources for that we may as well just give our parents the cash.

Merry squeezes her hands in front of her chest. "Sir, I'll bake you a pie to prove that it'll be a success."

"Your grandmother won the blue ribbon for her pies at least ten years running. I trust you know your way around dough." Marley juts his chin at me. "Tommy Costa, was it? Sounds Italian. I'm sure you know how to make pizza just fine and all—" Mr. Marley wags his finger between Merry and me as he speaks and then his cellphone rings, cutting him off. "I'm a busy man. Last chance. That's the executive from CoffeeHut. He calls me at least once a day because this is prime property. He wants to get his hot little hands on it. What should I tell him?"

Merry's sky-blue eyes open wide, imploring, but also fill me with the sense that anything is possible.

"We'll take it," I blurt. Then turning to her I say, "You're in, right?"

She swallows thickly and nods slowly.

"In that case, I'll have you sign the contract." He flips a piece of paper in our direction.

Seated at a small table together, knees so close I can feel the warmth from Merry's body, we browse the paperwork, sign, and hand over deposit checks.

As the door closes behind Marley, the dust seems to sparkle in the dim light.

Merry turns to me and says, "I just gave him all my savings, and it wasn't much. I thought I was broke before. Now, I'm beneath broke. Broker? Broked? Brokened?" Eyes still wide, she looks at me and says, "What did we just say yes to?"

The corner of my lip lifts in a smile. "I think we just agreed to give Hawk Ridge Hollow a pizza and pie shop that they'll love."

"That's optimistic." Merry slouches in the chair.

"You have a business plan, let's see it."

"It's for a pie shop."

"Pizza pie," I say in an imitation of a lilting Italian accent.

"It's not the same," Merry says, but her lips ripple with a faint smile.

"It's round, has dough, crust, filling."

"Tommy," she says in a way that transports me back to the time when we were a constant presence for each other in college.

When everyone else was experimenting with their identity, going to parties, and getting wild—don't get me wrong, I did a little bit of that—I was always happiest with Merry. That's why I call her that. We were comfortable together. Content. But just friends. Until one night after a basketball game, I thought that maybe there was a mutual spark.

Never mind. If we're going to be in business together, I have to keep things in the friend zone. Pals, chums, *amici*.

I cannot think about the way she bites her soft, pillowy lower lip, how she blinks slowly with those long lashes, and how gorgeous she looked in the gown at Cassie's wedding despite the frosting.

Friend zone.

I clear my throat. "Last night, after running into each other and the reminder that Hawk Ridge Hollow is your hometown, I was going to suggest we get together for coffee sometime."

"Or pie." She waves her hand vaguely, signaling we now have a shop together.

"I bet that would be delicious."

Merry leans forward. Despite my lung damage, I breathe in her sweet apple scent.

Pals.

"That this is a huge undertaking. I'm going to admit, coming over here this morning was more of a whim and less of a long-term, well-thought-out plan," she says.

I tap her binder and our fingers brush as she moves toward it, sending heat creeping up my arm and igniting my chest.

Chums.

I draw my hand away. "Your business plan would prove otherwise."

"You haven't seen or heard it yet."

"But I know you, Merry. Anything you've ever done, you do thoroughly, perfectly."

A sad smile flickers across her face. More than anything I want to soothe what upsets her and how she seems so...lonely.

"I've never done this." She points at me and then back to herself.

My heart leaps because for a second I think she means *us*. Sure, we were close back in college, but like a skipped question on an exam, we never answered whether there was something more between us.

But that was then. This is now. I can't let the possibility inspired by her beautiful sky-blue eyes make me think we could go back.

Amici.

I rub my hands together and say, "Merry, we have to do this." Then, with humility, I tell her about the predicament with my parents. "Sure, between the seven of us, we could probably each contribute to their financial resources and they'd be fine, but—"

This is the hard part to say because it's difficult to face, knowing that Ma and Pop, who are two larger-than-life personalities and always took care of us, need our help.

"But they wouldn't accept handouts. It would make them

feel..." I pause, searching for the right word. "Helpless. And like a burden and a whole host of other things."

Merry nods slowly. "When Nan's health declined, first when she fell then with the stroke, it was like that. Of course, my love and respect for her didn't change a bit, but I know that it was hard for her to face the changes. She prided herself on being independent. The contents of the binder are largely the ideas she talked about over the years for the bakery that she always wanted to open." Merry seems to shrink while she talks as if it's somehow her fault.

"But she never did? Any idea why not?"

She casts her gaze to the floor. "Nan got a job at the resort. They had good employee benefits. And, as you know, having to unexpectedly take care of my sister and me then losing my grandfather, I guess she had to put the bakery on the back burner, so to speak."

I want to reach out and hold her hand because I sense she somehow blames herself for her Nan's dream not coming to pass. "That's what we do for family. Just like how you left college to help her."

Her gaze lifts from the floor. "I guess I didn't think of it that way."

The corner of my lip hitches with a smile and I chuckle, once more, attempting to lighten the mood. "You said back burner. I hope we can keep things cool in the kitchen with plenty of puns."

She flashes me a flat look as if to say my kind of silly, dad-humor is awful.

I school my expression. "Right. Business. I also hope I'm doing the right thing," I say, meaning by my parents and with Merry.

She takes my hand, startling me. Hers is cold but soft. "You're a good son, Tommy. And I won't lie. This is an unexpected and unusual situation, but..." She glances out the window to where Christmas lights twist around the trees against the increasingly gloomy day. "But I don't see how we can make it work."

"Well—" I start, but the door flies open, cutting me off.

Merry startles and her hands fall away.

Frankie and her three kids stand in the entryway. She holds Rafael while Stella and Charlie tackle hug my legs.

"You were serious," Frankie says as if ready to rip into me. "Oh, hi Merilee. How are you?" she adds as if belatedly noticing the most beautiful woman I've ever laid eyes on.

"I'm interesting," Merry answers.

I agree. She's the most fascinating woman I've ever met. Plus, cute, clever, and caring. I could probably come up with a pun, but I'll save those for the nieces and nephews. At least I'll get a laugh out of them.

Frankie raises her eyebrows. "What's interesting is finding my brother in this dump."

"It has good bones, despite the dust. Lots of potential," I reply, paraphrasing what Mr. Marley told us.

"I mentioned your cockamamie idea to Tripp and Sadie. They thought this location was available but hinted that there are some property tax issues."

"Mama, you said caca," Charlie says with a giggle.

Merilee tries to hide hers.

Frankie gives a stern shake of her head to remind him to mind his manners. She looks so much like Ma I make a note not to use potty talk in front of my sister.

"Dallen would know about tax issues. I'll talk to him. In the meantime, welcome to the new pizza shop." I spread my arms wide then add, "And pie."

"Pizza pie. I love pizza pie," Stella says in her squeaky little girl voice.

I nod. "Me too, Stella-bella, but I meant pizza and pie. As in Miss Merry and I are going into business together."

Frankie's eyes bulge. "That's a twist. You ought to add soft serve while you're at it."

"Soft serve. I love ice cream," Charlie says.

"Oh, and her name is Merilee. Sorry about that," my sister apologies to Merry who looks on as if not sure what to make of the chaos that is but a small fraction of my family.

"Actually, it's *Merry*," I correct.

"Merilee," Frankie says, her fiery Italian temper flaring.

"Merry," I counter.

"Tomaso, I know Merilee Ketchum and her name isn't—"

"I know her too," I reply.

Frankie rocks back on her heels. "Oh. You do?"

"We went to college together." I leave off about how she abruptly left, and how it wasn't the same without her there. Like she took a part of me with her.

Frankie's expression changes from ready to charge me like an angry bull for getting the woman's name wrong to something else. Did I ever mention Merry to her or my other siblings?

The deep V between my sister's eyebrows disappears when Rafael pats her cheeks with his chubby hands. "Anyway, I was on my way to the supermarket to pick up some supplies for the storm that's coming and saw your truck parked out front, Tommy."

Merry glances at the big red beast with the knobby tires hulking in the parking space.

"Bryan—" Frankie starts.

"Bruno," I interject.

"He goes by Bryan now."

"What's with you two and names?" Merry murmurs.

"Bryan got Ma and Pop on a flight ahead of the storm. Nico will pick them up from the airport in about an hour, and then they'll be along right after." She speaks like an army commander preparing the troops.

"No! Na!" says Rafael, the youngest, and still learning to talk.

Stella corrects him, "Nonna and Nanno." I can see she'll grow up to be a lot like her mom, and chuckle because she'll give my sister a run for her money.

"Yes, they'll be here in a little while, and I do not want to be around when they find out why Uncle Tommy essentially had them abducted by their other son and sent halfway across the country," Frankie says in baby-talk but clearly directed at me.

"Well, this has been lovely. As usual," I say dryly to my sister. "Next time you guys come in here, there will be pizza and pie," I say to the kids, giving them each a bear hug back.

As Frankie and the crew leave, Merry looks on with longing and then shakes like she had snow in her hair. Thankfully, it hasn't started to fall yet. I wonder if there is a Mr. Merilee.

FRIEND ZONE. TOMMY. FRIEND ZONE.

"One down, five to go. As in, I have the other five siblings to convince this is a doable idea," I mutter more to myself than anyone else.

"In that case, we ought to get started." Merry opens her binder slowly like she's not sure whether she wants to move forward or if she fears she'll regret this.

I part the pages of the spiral notebook as if we're back in college, getting ready to study for a test when a piece of paper falls out, fluttering to the floor by Merry's feet.

We both move to pick it up. Our heads bump softly and our gazes float together for half a beat before she glances away and picks up the paper.

It's then I realize it's the marriage pact.

CHAPTER 5

MERILEE

Yanking my gaze loose from Tommy's, I tell myself that the tremble on my lips, the squeeze in my belly, and the warmth in his eyes don't mean anything. I pick up the loose piece of paper that fell out of a spiral notebook with a doodle of a cartoon version of us on the cover as popcorn explodes everywhere—reminding me of how popcorn truly was our inside joke. I vaguely remember the notebook from college.

I do a double-take when I see my name on the sheet of paper and definitely remember the details of the pact now.

Tommy goes to grab it from me, but I playfully clutch it to my chest.

I skim our writing. "This is a blast from the past. Thirty has come and gone, and then some. Crazy that we ever thought that was old. What were we thinking?" I try to laugh off the fact that if the way I'm feeling right now is any indication, my crush on Tommy Costa was colossal. As big as the Hawk Ridge mountain range. Too bad I didn't recognize it at the time.

He shuffles his boot against the dusty ground. "I meant to toss it out."

My chest craters. "Oh." I hold out the paper for him to take.

"I meant, it's silly. We were so young and—"

I can't deny that being with him again puts me on cloud five of nine. However, the dismissive comment drops me back to the rocky bottom. "Right. I understand."

I try to rearrange my expression into the cheerful, small-town girl version of myself that he knew back in college. Not the single, lonely, and increasingly hopeless small-town Merilee that I've become...who still has a mega crush on Tommy Costa, by the way. Also, totally not fair.

I can't help but sigh at the sad state of my non-existent love life.

"No, that's not what I meant. I just didn't want you to get the wrong idea." He grips the back of his neck.

Taking a deep breath, I shove my disappointment and sadness aside, down, and away. I'm here to make Nan's and my dream come true, whatever it takes. Enough people in this town have seen me floundering as I try to find my way, and I refuse to be seen as a failure. Not only that, but he's probably still the same old college goofball who could commit to little more than a slice of pizza or a movie.

"It's fine, Tommy. I get it. Really. It's not like I expected us to uphold a marriage pact after all this time. You probably found someone special and," I wave my hand, "if we're going into business together, we should have some rules too."

He glances at the paper. "Like first person here gets to control the radio, no secrets allowed, honesty always..."

I read over his shoulder, getting a deep breath of his spicy, masculine scent. "Smells good." My voice is far too breathy for afternoon conversation. "I mean, sounds good. That's what I meant."

His eyebrows pinch together with concern. "Actually, I was thinking this place was a bit musty and there's an odor coming from the bathroom area." He points toward a closed-door labeled

Restroom.

I step back and my nose automatically wrinkles because away from him, now, I smell it too.

"What I was about to ask is if you want to shake on it?" he asks, moving closer to me.

"We should write down the rules and sign a pact like before. While we're at it, we can tear up the old pact." My throat tightens as I speak those words.

But Tommy doesn't rip it in half and then stomp it into the dirty floor like I imagine myself doing if only to stamp out the longing for him that rises inside me like sunshine—something in short supply here in the mountains during the winter. I can't get my hopes up or let anything like desire bubble up because that's a surefire recipe for failure when it comes to business.

Instead, he tucks the pact back into his notebook and opens to a fresh sheet of paper. It occurs to me that despite what he'd said about the pact being silly, he never got rid of it. Does that mean anything?

Nadine's voice booms in my head, telling me not to be such a silly, hopeless romantic, and according to her helpless. I'm glad she never met Cassie. Together, they'd have the ability to ruin young women's dreams, especially mine.

Tommy writes down the rules we established and then abruptly gets to his feet. "If we're going to include the toilet seat rule like from the original pact, I should probably make note of whether there is a mister in your life."

The drafty room chills a degree or two. "A mister like a boyfriend or a husband?"

He nods sharply. "We'll have to create a business entity, and we ought to know if significant others factor in. What's your status? Are you married? Engaged? Dating?"

If I didn't know better, I'd think Tommy Costa was rambling nervously.

"Nope." I punctuate the word more forcefully than I mean.

"Single-serve string cheese over here." I raise my hand like a student in class during roll call.

"I love string cheese," he says offhandedly as if not grasping my meaning. "Anyway, for the record, there isn't a missus in my life. In case you were wondering." His tone shifts to smooth, flirty?

I'm not entirely sure, but the draft gives way to a gust of warmth as the awkwardness dissolves and hope returns.

Peeking up from the paper where I sign my name, I say, "Yes, I was wondering."

Tommy's eyebrow twitches with interest. "You were?"

"Well, yeah. As you said, the thing about business entities." My jaw trembles again.

"Not because of the pact?" he asks, stepping closer to where I sit.

I open and close my mouth, but no words form.

"Merilee Merry Ketchum, you signed this document and it includes total honesty." He taps our impromptu business pact.

I gasp. "You tricked me."

His lips quirk. "I didn't." He steps closer still, and like a ship navigating uncertain waters, I can almost see the moment he changes tack. "Here's the truth. I panicked when you saw that I still had the pact. The childish college kid inside, who was too scared to say how he really felt, didn't want you to think I was over here pining away. Then I realized we're not in college anymore."

"Does that mean you're pining away?" I say around a laugh because what's likely to be a breathy voice could reveal my true desire.

Why am I scared to hear him say exactly what I've wanted to —going on over a decade? What I've told myself could never be because of the incident between him and Cassie? I get to my feet, ready to run away because this suddenly feels intense, overwhelming.

He takes another step closer, and we're mere inches apart.

"It means we can be adults and not play silly games." His voice is imposing, gravelly.

Suddenly warm all over, even though the thermostat on the wall indicates this room is a freezer box, I snap my fingers because I was right. "See, I knew you thought the pact was silly. That I'm silly, nothing more than a small-town girl who—"

Tommy's espresso brown eyes capture mine. My pulse drums with each breath I take, with every word that he speaks, and what it could mean.

"A beautiful, small-town *woman* who I'm happy to have reconnected with after all this time. And you're not nothing. Merry, you're much, much more. Sure, we were young when we made the pact, but maybe it meant something—something our college selves couldn't discuss over coffee at the student center. Although, I do have a lot of good memories of us hanging out there and of our friendship."

The wind, even though it continues to blow outside, drops from my sails at the reminder that we're just friends.

However, Tommy continues and angles his finger to me then back at himself. "But the mature adults in the room are going to talk about how we really feel over pizza and pie."

The wind lifts again, outside too, and batters the striped awning. The aluminum thing lifts and then breaks away with a clatter as it knocks directly into the windshield of my car.

Gasping, I rush to the door, but Tommy grips my arm. Suddenly stone-cold serious, he says, "Hang on. The damage is done. Wait for the wind to die down. Don't want any flying objects to hit you."

"But my car."

"We can get it fixed."

"I have a small amount of savings left, mostly in the form of rolled coins. But I have to put it into this place. What am I going to do?" I wilt at the sight of how the metal frame of the awning impaled the glass.

"For now, we can rideshare to our place of employment. My sister mentioned the storm coming. Let's make a game plan for the shop, grab some supplies for the storm, and my brother and I will take care of your car so it's not towed when the town has to plow." My brain races to catch up to the guy who I remember as being my goofy college best friend to a man who takes charge, all business.

"Your brother lives here?" I recall a few visits to campus made by some configuration of the Costa guys, and remember their names, but cannot fathom how they found their way from the city to this tiny town.

"One for now—Luca. He's up at the cabin next to Frankie and Rusty's place. Nico is floating as usual."

"I didn't realize Frankie was your sister. I've only ever known her as Frankie Hawkins. She and Rusty must've gotten married when I was away on one of my attempts to leave Hawk Ridge Hollow behind. Small world."

"Small town." Tommy tells the story of his grandfather coming here and winning a cabin in a card game, the Christmas tree farm, Frankie moving into the place, and then a whirlwind international wedding afterward.

"What brought you here?" I ask.

"I, uh, got injured on the job." He shifts uncomfortably. "Had to retire. Saw an opportunity to invest here and be closer to Frankie and Luca. In addition to wanting my parents closer after being scammed, our family is scattered and I've been looking for something to bring us back together. To make Ma and Pop proud."

"That's really honorable." Never mind my family being scattered, Nan and Nadine were all I had left except a few far-flung cousins. I open the binder to the first page, and read, "'Why I want to open a pie shop: to honor my grandmother's memory and make her proud as well as create community and connect with people.'"

Tommy's brown eyes search mine because we have the same goal.

"Maybe this will work after all," I say.

"Did you ever doubt?"

"Yeah, right around when you said you don't have restaurant experience."

His shoulders shake with a laugh. "Thanks for your honesty."

"Always." Except for the colossal crush. For now, I'll keep that to myself.

"You ready to do this?" Tommy asks.

I flip on the overhead lights, illuminating the shop against the increasingly darkening sky. "That would be a yes."

We lose ourselves in the next hours as we pull the cloths off the furniture and fixtures, take inventory of what's here, and brainstorm how we can make pizzas and bake pies at the same time.

There I thought Mr. Marley was suggesting I go into business with a pimply pizza boy. As if. Tommy is quite the opposite—almost taller than I remember, broader in the chest, stronger, and he's grown nicely into his features. A study in tall, dark, and handsome like a work of Italian fine art.

"The old tables and chairs are in decent shape," Tommy says, examining them.

Broken from my thoughts, if anyone is pining, it's me. I try to organize a response. "If we get some tablecloths, they'll make do until we can afford new tables."

Even though we're moving around, it's cold in here. Then again, I'm always chilly. Involuntarily, I shift closer to Tommy.

"I like those classic red and white checkered tablecloths," he says, reminding me of the typical pizza shop style.

"For the pie shop, I envisioned sweet shades of pale pink, light green, and cream, but that won't suit a pizza parlor." Thinking of Cassie's wedding colors, I have an idea and search for what I have in mind on my phone. "What do you think of this palette?"

Tommy reads the names of the colors, "Burgundy brown, medium green, off white, and pumpkin. I could deal with that."

"Perfect. This place is filthy, but we can clean it up no problem."

"Nico will help. Luca will fix the broken glass. What else?"

We move to the counter area.

"When I was a kid, I remember coming in a few times with my grandfather and ordering over here." I stand toward the left where a lower cold case could hold pies and the upper area with glass shelves where pizzas were available to buy by the slice. "Then we'd pay over here."

Tommy pushes the button on an old-fashioned metal cash register. The drawer opens with a *ping*. Inside are a few paperclips, an arcade coin from a place that is no longer down the street, and some lint.

"Still works."

"That's promising." We move into the prep kitchen and Tommy holds his hands in front of the commercial-sized oven. "Flipped this thing on when you were in the front, and it's giving off heat. I'll bring some tools tomorrow and inspect the woodfire oven to make sure it's safe to use."

"I forgot you studied fire science. You must know Chief Hawkins."

"We've met a few times. Good guy. My knowledge comes in handy even though I'm no longer in the field." Tommy speaks heavily as if each word weighs as much as a commercial sack of flour. Then, as if moving on, he says, "Anything else?"

I edge toward the bathroom to make sure it's in working

order then leap back, and into Tommy's arms. They're strong and close protectively around me.

"What is it?"

With a shaky finger, I point to the bathroom. "It's...it's a...a blob."

Tommy's brow ripples as he slides in front of me and peers at the festering, greenish pink thing with black spots floating in the sink before coughing into his hand and slamming the bathroom door.

We reconvene in the dining room area and as far away from the offending odor as possible.

"It's not necessarily common knowledge, but firefighters do more than douse flames and rescue kittens from trees." He shakes his head slowly. "I've seen some gnarly things, but nothing like that."

"It was gruesome. But what was it?"

"Definitely a blob."

Expressions serious, our gazes meet then we both crack up with laughter.

"You think it was a blob? Really?" I ask when I catch my breath.

"Honestly, I have no idea. Maybe something backed up in the commode or is rotting in there. When I bought my house, I had to hire a plumber. I'll call him and see if he can get out here to have a look."

"If he dares."

"I'll suggest he brings a hazmat suit."

Despite the content of this discussion, Tommy's eyes float to mine. My jaw trembles slightly, but I try to hold his gaze and discover what's behind it. To not be afraid of my wishes coming true.

Are we picking up where we left off before the college dorm room Cassie calamity or after? As friends or with the crush chemistry that I only realized existed later, after I hyper-analyzed our relationship during long spans of solitude?

Tommy's lips quirk and his eyes sparkle.

Whatever is in the bathroom sink makes a gurgling sound. I startle, breaking the moment.

We laugh again, and when we stop, a smile rises on my lips that I'm sure matches Tommy's. It's like the smile we shared after the popcorn fiasco back in college and many times after that.

"You know, this is going to be a lot of work, but I don't think it's going to be all that hard," he says.

"Easy work, if there was ever such a thing." That was something Nan would say.

We make a list of what needs to be done and ordered then go over how to divide the duties and expenses. Just as we're about to lock up, a commotion comes from outside.

"I don't know. Frankie said he's here," a male voice calls over the wind.

A woman wearing a black wool jacket with a silk scarf over her head peers through the window. A stooped man shuffles behind a smaller version of Tommy—same dark hair, features, and full lips.

I shouldn't be thinking about Tommy's lips when I'm pretty sure his parents and brother are outside.

My new business partner lets out a sigh and opens the door with a grand swoop of his arm. "Ma! Pop! Welcome to the new pizzeria and pie shop!"

"What sun-forsaken place have you brought us to, son?" Mrs. Costa says.

"Is it always so windy?" Mr. Costa asks.

"The flight was delayed and then we hit turbulence," Mrs. Costa complains.

"And Nico here brought us to a pizza shop that's been closed down." Mr. Costa shakes his head distastefully.

"I'm starved," Mrs. Costa adds.

The man who'd previously been full of confidence and positivity deflates under their criticism. "Ma, Pop. Don't worry. You're going to love it here. This place is going to be amazing." He rifles off some Italian words and I recognize the ones that have to do with food, including mozzarella, parmesan, and pepperoni.

That reminds me of Marley's potential deal with the coffee or pizza chain and our deadline.

Mr. and Mrs. Costa don't look convinced by Tommy's enthusiasm.

"When you called and said you had a surprise, I hoped we were going to hear that you're finally getting married." Mrs. Costa clicks her tongue.

Mr. Costa says something in Italian, but instead of making me think of passionate stories of romance and delicious meals, I sense Tommy gets a scolding.

"None of our sons are married, and there I thought we were finally going to get good news." Mrs. Costa says as if this is the crime of the century.

"I do have good news, Ma."

She gives him the fiercest *mom* look that I've ever seen. "Tomaso, if I go to my grave not having attended your wedding, I promise I'll haunt you from the beyond. That goes for all of you." Her eyes flit to Nico.

"Don't look at me. I just work here," he says, swallowing thickly. "And since my brother is a menace in the kitchen, I'm not sure how long that'll last."

If I remember correctly, Nico is the youngest and a bit of a jokester.

As for Tommy, even though he's big and strong, handsome and brave, especially as a firefighter for all those years, he seems to shrink under his parents' scrutiny.

I wring my hands, desperate to do something to show them that this place will be great and make them proud of their son.

"Call us when you're finally going to man up and say, 'I do,'" Mr. Costa mutters.

"When there's a wedding to plan," Mrs. Costa adds.

"There is," I blurt.

They both turn to me, mouths hanging open, as if noticing me standing in the room for the first time.

CHAPTER 6

TOMMY

Forget pepperoni, my eyes must be as big as slices of salami when Merry announces to my parents that there is a wedding. Maybe I misheard.

"Whose wedding?" I mutter so only she can hear.

"Our wedding." She smiles brightly without breaking eye contact with my family.

A flurry of questions balance on my tongue, but then I recall the pact...and the pressure from my parents to be a good Italian boy and tie the knot.

Forget making my parents' day, they look at her like she's an angel from heaven who, in one daring statement, made all their dreams come true.

I open and close my mouth, not sure what to say or do.

If you were to use three words to describe my five brothers and me, they would be loyal, protective, and tough. Most of the time, I live up to that. Oh, and single. Yes, all six of us. Since Ma and Pop are from the old country, this is about as criminal as you can get. As for my sister, she's the youngest and a spitfire. I thought she was the opposite of Merry, but now I'm not so sure. That was a bold move. Brazen.

She slides her hand into mine. "That's right, there's going to be a wedding. Back in college, Tommy and I made a promise to get married before we turned thirty. As Tobias Marley says, 'Two heads are better than one. It's all or nothing. That's my best and final offer—'" Merry bites her lip as if to stop the runaway freight train ramble.

"We made a pact," I add.

In a whisper, she says, "Thanks. I'm not sure where I was going with that, but I hoped some of Marley's business savvy, convincing us to do this, would rub off."

I'm not sure I'd refer to it as savvy. More like abrupt and blunt orders.

My mother and father remain still, stunned, their eyes scanning the woman at my side.

"Who is Tobias Marley?" Pop asks. "I've always told you, be careful of advice from people you don't know, who don't do what you do. Until they've walked a mile in your shoes..."

Nico chuckles and says, "Dad, you've never told us that. You must be Merry." He steps closer and says, "I remember Tommy mentioning your name back when you were in college. Looks like you rekindled an old flame, eh?"

"And we're all getting older, and colder, by the minute. I hope your place has heat, Tomaso," my mother grumbles. "When is this wedding, anyway?"

I step behind both my parents, place a heavy hand on each of their shoulders, and begin to shuffle them toward the door. "My house sure does have heat and a big fieldstone fireplace. Also, this place has a woodfire oven. Just wait until we get it cranking. You'll think you're in the tropics."

"I'll believe it when I see it. Tell me more about this marriage pact," Ma says, eyeing us suspiciously. "If that's like an arranged marriage, I have some questions I'd like answered. Namely, do you expect a dowry? If so, I can't make any promises. Our money is tied up in Liegeria right now." She puffs up.

Again, I open and close my mouth not sure where to start because there was no logical beginning. This morning, I was hardly prepared to discuss my business proposal, yet here I am, a newly anointed pizza pie parlor owner-operator and engaged to be married. If I'm not careful, by the end of the day I'll be Pop's age.

"Tomaso, why didn't you tell us?" he asks.

"It all happened very fast," Merry says.

My sentiments exactly.

"There's no dowry. That's not how it works. It would be customary for the bride's family to provide one, but we're not doing that." Exasperation nips my words. "I, uh, didn't mention it because, as Merry said, the news is fresh out of the oven." My nervous laughter drops like pennies in a till.

Merry takes my hand and squeezes it. "It's been quite a flurry. I'm Merry—Merilee Ketchum. It's nice to finally meet you."

Nico whistles low. "Smells like desperation, bro." Only, he says it in Italian, to which I reply with an unkind word, also in Italian.

Pop raps me on the back of the head with his gloves. "None of that language, young man."

"Show them the pact," Merry says.

I present the business deal we signed.

Merry cocks her head. "The other one, Tommy."

"Right." I wince and show it to my parents not at all sure how this is going to pan out. They're traditional and the pact is about as unconventional as you can get. Then again, so is a pizza and pie parlor and here we are.

My mother takes her cheater glasses out of her handbag and reads it slowly under her breath, nodding a few times. "One of them is distasteful but fair enough. I've been married for nearly forty years and have six sons. Smart of you to include it," she says to Merry, presumably referring to the rule about farts. Ma passes my father the pact along with the cheater glasses.

"Where are your glasses, Pop?" I ask.

He slides on the cheaters and holds the paper at arm's length. "Your mother and I share now."

"Don't tell me you gave them to the Liegerian prince," Nico says.

"No, of course not. A nice fellow in the subway station was having a tough time reading the map. I let him borrow my glasses."

"You never got them back, did you?" With my hands on my hips, I gaze at the ceiling and shake my head.

"The prescription glasses Gio got you?" Nico asks. "Those were a designer brand."

"What do I need with designer glasses? Your mother and I share everything. That's good enough for me."

Nico clucks his tongue. "Hopefully, not everything." He points to the item in the pact about the toothbrush.

"Come back and talk about it when you've been married for nearly forty years." My father turns his attention to the pact. "Anyway, this checks out. Where do we sign?"

I brush my hand over my forehead. "You don't sign, Pop. In fact, don't sign anything unless I'm with you. As for the pact, Merry and I signed it in college. It was just a—" I'm about to say silly thing we did when we were younger. The college kid in me wants to defend my pride, but I stop short as I recall how Merry seemed to deflate when I commented on it being silly earlier. "It was just a blessing in disguise. An unexpected surprise."

I glance at Merry and her smile slowly appears as if relieved I caught on.

My mother tucks the glasses away and then with all five feet of her motherly Italian ferocity, she steps forward. "Your father and I agree to stay here as long as you get married by Christmas."

"By Christmas?"

"That's right."

"But Frankie is having a baby."

"The more the merrier. I don't want to have to wait around for you to grow your family either. You want kids, right?" my mother asks Merry.

From behind my mother, so she can't see, I give two thumbs up and nod rapidly, mouthing, *Answer yes*. Then I tilt my head to indicate we'll discuss it later.

"Yes, actually. I've always wanted a big family," Merry says then eyes me and nods almost imperceptibly, at least I think so.

My eyebrows creep toward my hairline. Looking back, I recall her in college mentioning she wanted to have a big family someday and joked that too bad she couldn't get a degree in motherhood.

Frankie has already provided three grandkids with another on the way. You'd think that would be enough for my parents though. I've never been competitive with my sister, but definitely compete with my five brothers. I suppose it wouldn't be the worst thing for Merry and me to get married before them especially considering I'm the oldest.

We can figure out the other stuff later.

"Son, you have your hands full with this new enterprise and a wedding to plan." Turning to my future fiancée, she leans close and says, "Now, Merry, I understand that you bake pies?" Leave it to my mother to want to discuss food. "I saw a fascinating seven-tiered wedding pie on a television program."

Suddenly overwhelmed by Ma's comment as the two seem to conspire about baking, my cheeks puff with a long exhale as I plop down into a chair. I have to admit that I fell head over heels for my best friend. Unfortunately, Merry never knew that. Then Cassie happened. That's something we're going to have to discuss before we get to love and marriage and babies in a baby carriage. And this shop...and the wedding.

It's then that I notice Merry is missing.

"I'm hungry. Nico, you were telling us about some kind of bread over at the Falcon and Horn?"

"It's called the Hawk & Whistle, Pop," Nico says. "We'll get something to eat and let these kids untangle this fascinating web they've woven."

I slug his upper arm.

"Ow, Tommy. What was that for?"

"You know what." My lips form a thin line.

"But I'm not wrong, am I?"

I scrub my hand down my face. "I have no idea. It's been a day."

"Then we'll leave you to it."

"I'm going to stock up for the storm, bring Merry home, and then move her car. Care to give me a hand after you get Ma and Pop settled at my place?" I ask my brother, pointing out the window at the awning that speared her car's windshield.

"Whoa. It has been a day," Nico agrees.

"You have no idea."

It takes at least ten minutes for us to say goodbye. My parents inevitably loop us back into conversation after we've said our parting words, and then they start up again, asking questions ranging from the firmness of the mattress in the spare bedroom at my house to the kind of yeast I plan to use for the pizza dough to making sure that we invite the Bettinelli's since Frankie accidentally forgot to include them on the guest list for her wedding.

"Ma, they're both over ninety, do you really think they're going to travel all the way here from Italy?"

"They went to Alaska last year, so I don't see why not," Pop says.

"It's just as cold here, I imagine." My mother wraps her scarf tightly around her head.

"See you in a bit," Nico says, bracing himself for the full onslaught of Ma and Pop Costa's undivided attention.

When they leave, a door opens next to the bathroom opens and Merry peers out. "Is the coast clear?"

"Are you okay? What's behind door number two? Hopefully, not another blob."

She wrings her hands and says, "I needed a minute because of the thing I said to your parents."

I peer over her shoulder to a closet-sized office, barely big enough for both of us. With one foot on the floor and the other bracing a stack of boxes, she balances precariously. Papers and supplies cover every surface and fill every shelf.

I extend my hand for her to take. "We'll figure it out."

She frowns. "Looks like we have our work cut out for us."

"And a wedding to plan," I say, laughing it off.

She remains still, eyes wide, gazing into mine like we're facing down a Yeti in a snowstorm, which wouldn't surprise me up here in northern Montana.

I tilt my head closer. "Thank you for trying to rescue me from the ongoing parental pressure to provide Ma with grandkids."

She nods and shakes her head. "Seriously, what have I done?" She fists my shirt. "Tommy, I'm sorry. I don't know what came over me. They were harassing you about the shop and marriage. It just—word salad came out of my mouth without my thinking. I don't know how, but I'll fix this and explain to your parents that we're not actually getting married."

I sink back slightly, feeling as gray as the outside sky that Merry wasn't suddenly overcome with the desire to stick with me in sickness and health, for better or worse. Through pizza and pie. "Let's take one step at a time."

A line forms between her eyebrows. "But I feel like we're two kids with big ideas but no plan."

"We have a plan. First, we have to go to the store and get some supplies for the storm. Then take care of your car. Next, there's the pizza and pie shop to get up and running. Everything after that, we'll handle as it comes," I say, my voice surprisingly steady even though inside it's like deep forces inside the earth shift the Hawk Ridge mountains.

Truth is, I don't mind the idea of marrying Merilee Ketchum. Not at all. But how can I tell her that without scaring her off?

Her spine lengthens. "You have a point. Wouldn't want to lose this place to a chain coffee shop or Signori Pepperoni."

"That's more like it. Trust me. We can make this work," I say, but I'm not sure if I mean the shop, our phony wedding pact, or all of it.

The thing is, if I want to convince her to actually marry me, I have to prove that I'm an adult and not the wishy-washy college kid that she knew, the one that was too afraid to tell her how I felt.

"I'm relatively new to Hawk Ridge Hollow. I know the basics, but how do you brace for a storm?" I ask as we bundle up to head outside.

"I could use some pie baking supplies. You know, so I can test some more recipes."

"Do you need a taste tester? Quality control?" No doubt, I wear an impish grin.

"Are you volunteering?"

"Free slices of pie? I'll gladly make the sacrifice of my time and tastebuds for you, Merry."

As we step outside, snowflakes start to fall, reminding me that this is a season of miracles. I *need* one for this pizza and pie shop to work. I *want* one to marry Merry.

While we drive over to the market, she tells me that the

storms in Hawk Ridge Hollow have been known to snow people in for days so it's smart to stock up on sundries.

"Don't get me wrong, your truck seems like it can handle it. Everyone here has four-wheel drive, chains, or studded tires, and the plows do a good job clearing the snow, but when those northern gales come, it can snow for days on end."

"Sounds bleak. I don't recall reading that particular fine print when I signed up to live here."

"You get used to it and learn to stay prepared. Also, afterward, it makes for great skiing."

"Aside from the wedding, I have yet to go to the resort."

"That means you're already a local."

"What do you mean?"

"We love the Hawk Ridge Hollow Resort, but during the high season, we leave it to the tourists and take advantage of their offerings on Tuesday afternoons when it's slow or non-winter break weekends when it isn't as crowded. And stay away during December, it's a mob scene."

"Ah, smart to finesse the system," I say with a chuckle, enjoying this time with Merry.

We head into the market, bustling with people prepping for the storm. She pauses in front of a display for the "Twelve *Deals* of Christmas."

"That pasta dish looks good," I say, pointing over her shoulder. "If only I could get my mother to release her recipe secrets. She keeps them under lock and key. I don't think even my father knows what she puts in the food she makes—he mostly slices, dices, and mixes, following her instructions."

Merry turns around and taps her chin. "Sounds delicious, but I was just thinking about something."

"Never shop on an empty stomach. Then you'll want one of everything."

She giggles. "True, but I had an idea. My Nan never opened a pie shop because she said she wouldn't make any money. She had a bad habit—or good, depending on how you think about it—of giving away her pies for free."

"Sounds like a generous woman."

"Definitely. What if every year we do something like that. Like this." She points to the "Twelve Deals of Christmas" sign. "But instead, it's the 'Twelve *Dishes* of Christmas.' In other words, we'll give a pizza or pie to twelve families or places in need.

"Merry, that's brilliant. After all, it's the season of giving."

"Nan also always said you have to give to get." She paces in front of the display. "Let's see. We can alternate, pizza and pie. There's Mr. Marley. He could use some Christmas cheer. A pizza would make the workers at the animal shelter over on Morris Avenue happy."

"What about the care home? Hawk Ridge Hollow Helpers, I think it's called."

"Wonderful idea. Clive loves pie. Be warned, he might fight you for my hand in marriage—carried over from his crush for my nan."

A little zip blows through me, but it's not at all cold like the wind outside. "Hmm. Sounds like I'd better be cautious. Older gentlemen really know how to woo the ladies."

Merry titters. "The guy who runs the Christmas tree stand has been swamped too."

"That's my brother, Luca."

"No way. He might like one."

"Doubtful. He's not a fan of the holiday." Like me with the accident, he's gone through a rough patch. If only he would talk about it.

"Ironic that he sells Christmas trees."

I grunt. "It's a good excuse to live a lonely man on the mountain life."

"There are always a couple of families at the church who could use a warm meal or dessert along with the firemen and police officers at the new safety complex. Also, I'm friends with Brynn at the school. They'd be happy to have a pizza luncheon for the teachers."

"A pie would brighten my mailman's day. He recently encountered a bear on his route."

"Yikes. Gwen Lawson is housebound, and I bet a pizza and a visit would mean a lot to her."

"That leaves us with one more to make twelve," I say.

"Well, there's Old Man Orson on the ridge. When I was a kid, we'd go sledding up there until he'd inevitably chase us off the hill." Merry shivers. "There were stories of him having captured Big Foot...and being Big Foot. The man was terrifying."

"Maybe a pie would soften him up. I love sledding."

She bumps me with her hip. "I suppose bringing him a preemptive peace offering isn't a bad idea."

I rub my hands together. "So we're going to do this? Twelve Dishes of Christmas. Looks like this business arrangement is already working out."

There's just one problem. I don't know how to make pizza.

CHAPTER 7

MERILEE

I add three sacks of flour and a brick of butter to the cart then go back for one more.

"Ahead of a storm, some people stock up on necessities like batteries and canned goods. I see that you're going for the butter," Tommy says, looking at the contents of other shoppers' carts as they walk past us.

"Better to be safe than pie-less." I don't mention that I'll be doing a lot of stress baking while trying to figure out how to run a business...and being engaged to Tommy.

He tips his head back with laughter. "If that means I get to benefit then I guess I shouldn't complain."

"A pie for a pie. By the way, I don't remember you making pizza back in college, though eating it was a different matter." I cast him a sharply raised eyebrow, recalling how he could house the stuff.

"I considered it an academic study, a minor in pizza-ology." He waggles his eyebrows.

This time I laugh. "There was that great place a few streets over from your dorm. But from all those so-called tests you conducted, eating slices, you did learn how to make it, right?"

Tommy winces. "I was a bit of a kitchen menace, but I know my way around flour, salt, yeast, and baking soda."

This time I raise both eyebrows. "Pizza dough does not contain baking soda."

He winks. "I was testing you."

"Is that so?" I narrow my eyes, playfully suspicious.

"Sure. How hard can it be?"

"Tommy, please tell me you know how to make pizza dough?"

"How about you teach me?" I get his flirty half-smile.

I slap my hand to my forehead and go to the baking aisle and grab some extra flour and yeast, just in case we have a disaster on our hands.

Back in the truck, I turn up the volume on the radio per the pact rule that the passenger gets to control the dial. To my surprise, he had it tuned to the local station that started playing Christmas carols right after Thanksgiving. We drive less than a mile out of town, leaving behind the Christmas decorations.

"That's me." I point to a modest craftsman-style house on the corner, trimmed with colorful lights.

"Of course, this is where you live." He chuckles.

"What's funny about it?" I ask, suddenly self-conscious.

"Merry, I remember in college you telling me that you missed helping decorate the gingerbread house. I didn't know you meant an actual house."

Funny, how much can get lost in translation. "Oh, you haven't seen anything yet." I describe the lit-up candy canes that'll line the front path, giant candy garlands, life-size gingerbread people, and evergreen swag covered with what looks like dripping icing. "I get the regular lights up the day after Thanksgiving to beat the snow then add in the rest later. My grandparents started the tradition. A few of the streets around town vote on holiday themes for all the residents on the block. We have gingerbread cornered. But it's fun to see what the others come up with."

"It's adorable," Tommy says slowly. "Like you."

The Christmas lights illuminate the inside of the truck, betraying my pink cheeks. I'm not accustomed to compliments, at least that's what I think that was. Even though I've gone so far as to ask Santa to wrap me up a husband for Christmas, hearing Tommy talk that way about little 'ole me makes me feel squirmy. I feel all kinds of awkward, like those times when you don't know where to put your arms even though you've had them all your life, so they've been *somewhere* all this time.

So what do I do? I bow. Yep. You heard it here folks. While seated, I do a clumsy little bow and nearly bash my nose into the armrest between us.

Tommy's expression filters from confusion to amusement.

The Merilee he knew was cool, calm, collected. Not cool like Cassie or my sister. Cool like usually chilly. Sure, I may have had an itty bitty crush on him, but I was mostly oblivious to how I felt at the time.

Ignorance is bliss and all that.

He cracks a smile and continues, "And bold, brave, confident. To walk into the midst of the Costa family and form an alliance, make a treaty...when I've been battling with them about marriage."

Oh, so he's just joking around. The tension lessens but so does my hope that something more can develop between us even though I have no idea how to navigate it. I banter back the way we always did because this, I know how to do.

"Ha ha. Just call me General Ketchum."

"The real war we're going to have to fight is with the blob in the bathroom." Tommy wiggles his fingers in my direction like it's going to attack me.

I return the gesture and our hands brush, casting a tingle

through me. "If so, you have to rally the troops to go head to head with the thing."

Our fingers link. Tommy's eyes pour into mine, my cheeks go a shade redder. Even though this is exactly what I want, I'm not sure how to respond. I didn't study Flirting 101 the same way he did with pizza back in college. So I resort to what I know how to do: being the silly, fun friend. It's better, safer to pick up where we left off.

"What if the blob has cooties? I can't get married to a guy with cooties."

"As I said, I'll be calling the plumber." He goes quiet and a beat passes. "Merry, I'm proud to say you're my partner." His voice turns low, husky.

Like when combining wet and dry ingredients during baking, the lines between friendship and fake relationship blur. Despite me announcing the marriage pact, I can't let that happen because when we tell the truth, I'll be the one left with the broken, blobby heart.

"I'd like to propose an amendment to our pact. Our Bill of Business, if you will. We shall never mention the blob again." I hold out my hand to shake because there's nothing like being a goofball to try to diffuse the self-conscious discomfort brought on by the way Tommy looks at me with his dark eyes. And even though I have no idea what I'm doing and likely fumbling, resulting in an *F* in the grade book, I want his touch. I want more of him, of us.

His hand slides into mine. The callouses on his palm and fingers are rough against my skin, but in a way that makes me feel safe and like he can do anything. Hopefully, that includes tossing pizza dough. Instead of a surge of excitement, the calm comfort I seek soothes me.

Our gazes float together, and I let out a breathy little sigh as the dough and lines blend and cross, creating a mess in my internal kitchen.

Tommy's phone, resting on the console between us, beeps. The word *Fratelli* lights up the screen.

"That would be the group chat with my brothers. Hopefully, our parents didn't send more money to the Liegerian prince."

"I should head in any way." Inviting Tommy to join me stands on the tip of my tongue, but I hold back. We'll have plenty of time together in the coming days.

"Nico and I will take care of your car too. I'll pick you up first thing in the morning."

"Thanks again for everything, and my apologies for telling your parents that we're getting married. I overstepped. That was wildly inappropriate of me."

"Was it?" he asks.

I wave my hand dismissively. "I didn't want your mother to haunt you. Friends have to look out for each other and their parents' ghosts. And I was swept up, wanting to make sure the pizza and pie shop works out—we have got to come up with a better name. That does not roll off the tongue. Pie-ology is good, but I worry that people won't get it. Hmm..." I tap my chin.

"You're rambling again." His lips quirk. "It's cute."

Kill me now. Never mind. I've already died of mortification. Why am I so cringy? Then his second comment catches up with me. "I'm cute?"

His half-smile and slow nod are the stuff of my dreams. Cloud nine, I'm coming up.

"You sure are, Merry."

Alert! Alert! My cheeks are going up in flames. Although, Tommy is a former firefighter, perhaps he can help. On second thought, no-can-doozies. If he's the cause, it's unlikely he can provide a solution.

Oof. I drop my face into my hands.

"You don't have to be nervous," he adds, peeling my fingers away. "We'll figure this out."

The heat spreads to my neck and cheeks. I'm done for.

"Right. Yeah. Of course. New territory, being partners and all." I throw the truck's door open, wishing the snowbanks that I want gone by January first were already here so I could plunge my blazing head into the cold heap. No such luck. At least not yet.

"See you tomorrow," Tommy calls as I dash inside.

"Yes. Tomorrow. I'll be there. Here, I mean, since my car. Never mind." I seal myself inside the house, catching my breath. Not because the run was far or particularly taxing. Rather, I need to brush up on how to act like a normal human in front of an attractive and charming man.

Then again, this isn't college anymore. I've traveled all over the world, installed water wells in Africa, taught children to read in Ecuador, and took care of my ailing grandmother for several years.

I've proven that I know how to be an adult...and bake pies.

If I can make this work, I'll be able to share my pies with the people in Hawk Ridge Hollow. Finally owning a business is my dream come true and means I'll be able to contribute to the community and honor Nan's memory. I'll have a career and purpose. Despite the little pizza-shop-shared-space hiccup, the bakery will be welcoming, cozy, and a place locals and visitors alike will want to visit.

I can pull this off. I have to, especially since Tobias Marley now has my paltry savings for a deposit and rent money. My resolve strengthens and then goes down the drain while I take a cool shower.

Rehashing everything I said while with Tommy throughout the day, every move I made, and how much I embarrassed myself in front of him makes my cheeks flare up again.

I close my eyes, letting the water wash over me. With it comes the memory of coming home from college during break and Nan asking me about my classes and friends...and if there was someone special.

I told her there was a cute guy, but that we were just friends.

Friends that ate a lot of pizza together, studied, waited for each other after class, watched movies on the weekends, and went to school events together. Nan's smile blooms in my memory as if she knew that we also made haircut appointments at the same time, he took me to renew my driver's license, and we'd go shopping together like we did earlier this evening.

In other words, Tommy and I did all the things that best friends *and* couples do but without the label and the other benefits.

A benefit we came very close to experiencing. Once, in the library, his lips were so close to mine I thought we'd kiss. It was like sunshine on my skin. Then Cassie appeared—I didn't know she had any idea where the library was on campus. Her eyes widened as she possibly assumed that perhaps we weren't just friends after all.

Then the thing that burned itself into my wails like a fire alarm. I should've pulled it on my way out of the dorm room after I saw them together. Ironic, considering Tommy's former profession.

All of that aside, I'll admit that it was really nice holding hands with him earlier even if under the guise of me spouting off about how we're getting married. As if he'd want to marry me.

Although, he didn't protest and throw me out on the street or even refute the claim, telling his parents that I was drunk on pie so whatever I said while under the influence was unreliable.

I cup my hands over my face, mortified all over again. Why did I say that? Questions about what's wrong with me batter my mind.

Maybe I don't do my best thinking in the shower.

I dry off, wrap my hair in a towel, put on pajamas with snowflakes, and tie on my fluffiest robe. I could read one of the many romances I devour by the week, but I'd rather bake a pie. It'll relax me, smell good, and we'll need sustenance to begin work on the new shop tomorrow.

However, my bag of groceries from the market isn't here. I must've forgotten it in the truck when I fled.

The truth arranges itself in my mind like the sticks of butter and other pie baking supplies I'd purchased. Tommy and I picked up where we left off all those years ago—before everything that happened with Cassie.

When we'd started sitting closer together while in classes.

When we'd share bites of whatever we were eating.

When we'd snuggle while watching movies.

When we'd written the pact, but were both too scared to make a move. But why?

I drop into Nan's chair at the kitchen table as I recall what I'd told her when she'd asked if Tommy wanted to join me the next time I came home. With a gleam in her eye, she said she wanted to meet him. At the time, I thought that it wasn't a good idea for us to be boyfriend and girlfriend because it could change our perfectly good friendship. Then I erased the memory and notion from my mind as if I'd had amnesia, only remembering now.

But would that have ruined it? If we're picking up where we left off, will that lead us together after all?

There is the issue of what happened with Cassie. Then again, in a strange twist, we reunited at her wedding.

I take a deep breath, processing this as someone knocks on the door, startling me from my thoughts.

Turning on the porch light, Tommy stands under its glow wearing a dark green parka with a faux-fur-lined hood. Snow flurries behind him, wild in the night. His dark eyes, sparkling with mirth and mischief, transport me back to our college days.

We'd often go on adventures—just the two of us in our own little world. I suppose, the pizza and pie shop along with the prospect of marriage—and how to fix that fib—is the biggest adventure yet.

My pulse takes off, carrying my chill with it. I'm suddenly sweating in my pajamas even though my shower went long because I didn't want to get out and face the relatively cool house. If it's not summer, I'm probably shivering.

I still routinely ask myself why I live in one of the coldest places in the country.

When Tommy and I were in school, I said we were just friends. Then when I saw him with Cassie, the hurt I felt told me it was more than that. Much more.

I had a crush on Tommy.

I was mistaken before. The crush is bigger than the Hawk Ridge Hollow mountain range.

And, apparently, it didn't go away.

CHAPTER 8

TOMMY

I hold up the shopping bag from the trip Merry and I took to the market. "Forget something?"

"I just realized I'd left it behind when I was getting ready to bake a pie." Her breath puffs a cloud in the cold air.

"Firing up the oven at this hour?" I raise an eyebrow as a thought lifts in my mind.

She bundles her fluffy like pink robe tighter around her chest. "It'll warm up the house."

"If that's the case, is it too late to teach me how to make pizza crust? I belatedly realized it's a vital part of the enterprise."

She taps her finger on her chin. "You did, huh? That would've been something to have mentioned to Tobias Marley. Or, you know, me."

"Then I wouldn't have found myself in business with the best pie baker in Hawk Ridge Hollow."

"Ah, so the whole pizza thing was a ploy to rent out a filthy, moldering, former pizza place containing a questionable blob so you could learn how to make dough?"

"Yep. It's not the part about working with you as I said. I just want to make dough." I make finger guns and point at her to emphasize how she dodged another compliment.

She wags her finger at me. "Ah, I see. Dough like money. Good one."

I blow on the barrel of my finger gun. "Ah, just realized, you broke a rule. Remember the amendment you made? No mention of the you-know-what."

She winces. "Oops. Is there a fine that I'll have to pay? Bail to post?"

"I'll take the pizza dough lesson as payment."

"You drive a hard bargain, Tommy Costa." She steps aside and gestures that I come in.

Her house smells sweet, like butter, sugar, and years of baking.

Merry's eyes bulge as she pats her head, realizing her hair is in a towel. Like when she fled from the truck, she makes to run away, but I grab the tie to her robe and then reel her in.

"Wait a sec. Not so fast. Where are you off to?"

"Hair. Towel. Blob," she blurts.

I chuckle. "Ah. You broke the rule again. Pizza dough and...hmm. I'll have to think of another payment befitting your crime."

"Tommy, I'm in my pajamas and you look like this." She does a little shake of her hand in my general vicinity.

"This old jacket? Eh. Hardly my best. I have to admit the suit I had on the other night looked pretty sharp though," I say with false bravado. Formalwear is not my go-to, but when in Rome...and at weddings. "But why is *this* a problem?" I gesture to her evening attire.

"Because you're here," she stammers.

My pulse drums at how adorable Merry is. The fact that she cares about what she looks like in front of me gives me hope. So do her sky-blue eyes. So does her welcoming me inside.

A lot has changed since college, but not the fact that I like her. Definitely even more so.

"If you recall, I'd popped by your dorm plenty of times with you in various stages of dress—pajamas, sweaty athletic gear, dolled up and ready for all those fancy dinner dates you'd go on."

She balks. "I never went on fancy dinner dates."

"We ought to do something about that." I can't help but smirk because flirting with Merry makes her blush and comes as easy as...pie.

Her mouth slowly drops open. "I'm going to—" She points down the hall, presumably toward the bathroom where she'll brush her hair.

"In that case, I'll find the kitchen and an apron."

I'd spent plenty of time in Merry's dorm room, complete with a massive photo collage she and Cassie made, but being in her home is different. It's like I'm getting a peek behind the curtain. This is her personal space not shared with anyone.

A few vestiges of décor from another decade remain—some lace doilies, floral accents, and a rust-colored knit tea cozy. I think of how much she loved her grandmother. However, much of it shouts *Merry* from the colorful mixing bowls in the dish rack to the sunflower salt and pepper shakers.

There's nothing especially cohesive about the style like you'd find in an interior designer's showroom. Rather, it's all Merry—bright, cheerful, and tidy. Like her personality, her house is the kind of place where you want to hang out. It's comfortable, lived-in, and welcoming.

I wander to the fridge, covered in multiple wedding invitations. I count at least eight from this year. I linger on an adorable photo of mini Merry with pigtails and beaming a smile. She stands between her grandparents, holding each of their hands. Another, later with them seated at a table in a restaurant next to her sister. Merry wears a hat with bows on it while blowing out a candle. Nadine pouts as if jealous the attention isn't on her. There are a few more through the years. Then I spot one tucked partway behind a grocery list. It's of Merry and me sitting in the bleachers at a college basketball game. Her gaze trains on the camera, and mine is on her.

I become intensely aware of my heartbeat because the look is one of adoration, affection. Love?

Do I still love Merry as much as I did in college?

The answer comes to me swiftly. It's simple. In Italian, we say *Si*.

While at the market, I'd realized that Merry and I returned to our college low-level flirting status, practically picking up where we left off before Cassie attacked me, and then Merry departed early from school. That is, we'd resumed flirting until she realized what we were doing, then she got nervous. At least, I think so. But I can't figure out why she resists it other than the Cassie thing, but nothing happened between us. I wasn't interested. Made that clear. End of story.

Moments later, Merry returns, blonde hair brushed smooth and still in her robe as if trying to convince herself that she actually doesn't care what she's wearing in front of me.

I don't mind. Not a bit.

"How are your parents holding up?" she asks.

"After bringing your car to the repair shop—they said they'll have the new windshield in tomorrow morning—I went home to make Ma and Pop dinner."

"I thought you said you were a menace in the kitchen."

"Nico said that." I cough into my hand. "I confess that I've set a few things on fire. Pro tip: always keep an extinguisher handy."

"This doesn't bode well."

"Let it be known that I didn't only learn how to put out fires and rescue people when I was still with the fire department." My chest tightens when I talk about my calling, my career, but in the past tense.

"You were also a chef on the side but somehow didn't learn how to make pizza crust?"

"I'd like to say it's another ploy to get in the kitchen with you, but yes, given our shift rotation system, one of us would always cook for the other guys. Sadly, if I made pizza, it was with a store-bought crust. For the new pizza parlor, it's homemade or nothing."

"Then we agree on the level of quality and our commitment to customers."

I'm hoping we'll start to agree about a lot of things.

"Anyway, I had set a nice meal on the table, called Ma and Pop into the dining room, and found them both asleep with the television on. Ironic that it was a cooking contest."

"Well, roll up your sleeves, prepare to be amazed and astounded, then have to wait for the dough to rise. That's why I prefer pie dough. Instant gratification except if it needs to be chilled."

"Does that mean I'll have to be patient? Delay gratification?"

"Yep."

"Sounds familiar." Sounds an awful lot like us.

Cheeks taking on a soft shade of pink, Merry turns and stretches to reach the shelf above her kitchen cabinets to get a large bowl. She's on tiptoe, flicking her fingers to tip it forward as she struggles to get it down.

I slide behind her, inhaling her fresh apple scent, and say, "Let me help."

As my fingers close around the bowl, Merry loses her balance and teeters backward into me. In one swift movement, I set the bowl down and steady her. Caged between my arms, she turns around and we're face to face. I loop my thumbs in the belt of her robe, keeping her close.

"I'm not as tall without shoes on," she says, breathily.

She's plenty tall. I think about her long legs and hourglass figure hidden under her robe then inhale sharply. I'm equally taken by her smooth features, full lips, and those sky-blue eyes. If I leaned forward a few inches, my lips would be on hers—starting right up where we'd left off with an almost-kiss in the library years ago.

"We should probably get started," Merry says, snapping her gaze away from mine.

Instead of stepping aside, I linger there with her between my arms a minute longer, teasing the moment to see if she'll put aside her nervousness and let what started back in college continue to unfold.

The rosy glow deepens on Merry's cheeks, and she ducks out from under my arm. I lean against the counter and cross my legs at the ankles, wondering just how long it'll be before she gives in to whatever this is. But the better question is why is she resisting what we both so clearly feel?

The insecurity that appeared after the fire that changed my life, ending my career, flares up. I nudge it away like a pesky fly then fold up my sleeves and give my shoulders a shrug to adjust the fit of my button-down shirt.

I glance up as Merry blinks slowly as if in a trance or tired. I'm not entirely sure.

"You good?" I ask.

"So good." She wears a dreamy, ate too much pie on Thanksgiving, expression then clears her throat as if shaking it off and says, "Where am I? I mean, where was I?"

"Pizza dough."

"Oh."

For the next ten minutes, Merry gives me a science lesson on fermentation, yeast, and how it's a living organism. We make careful measurements and mix.

Then for a full minute, she plies the dough, kneading it rhythmically, purposefully. "Your turn. Give it a try."

I grip the dough which looks a lot smaller between my hands and try to imitate her motions.

"That's a bit too heavy-handed. Try a softer grip so you don't risk overworking the gluten." She smooths out the flour on the counter.

I try again.

Merry interrupts attempt number two. "You're not trying to squeeze the life out of the thing. Think of it like a caress as you push it away then a cuddle as you draw it near."

My hands go still on the dough. "A caress and a cuddle, huh?" Does she realize what she's doing to me?

I try again, but she stops me a third time. Never mind a hundred-pound firehose when empty, I'm used to handling them live while wearing about fifty pounds of gear. Er, was. I'm not built for a gentle touch, except perhaps when it comes to Merry.

"You'll have to give me a hands-on demonstration." I don't hide my smirk.

With a light grip, she closes her hands around mine which still holds the dough. "Yes, you have to be firm, but you're not trying to destroy the yeast." Her voice drops slightly.

Her hands on mine are so soft that I give in to a more tender approach.

"There you go. Now you're getting the hang of it." She draws back and says, "And that, sir, is payment for my earlier slip-up about the you-know-what."

I tip my head back with laughter. Merry isn't oblivious to what's happening between us, but she won't let herself fully buy-in. Still, she got me there, confirming that I wanted her to cross the boundary, and I'm okay with that.

"We can't over knead it, otherwise, we'll miss the real fun of tossing it, but first, we have to wait for it to rise." She sets a timer.

"And what'll we do while we wait?" I haven't flirted in nearly ten years. My brothers call me the "Anti-flirt" and never want me as a wingman. I'd inevitably and accidentally say or do something to shut down the prospective date they had their eye on.

"We bake a pie." Merry gets out another bowl and adds a combination of flour and other dry ingredients then cuts in the butter.

We chat while she rolls the dough into a thin sheet and then fits it into a dish with a scalloped edge.

I could sit here and watch this woman all day. It's not that I want her to work only so I can enjoy the fruits of her labor. Rather, it's the way she moves, with grace and intention, confidence and calm.

"This isn't a pie, technically. Inspired by the snow we're sure to have by morning, it'll be a blackberry tart with a sprinkling of sugar to make the berries look like they're glistening."

"Sounds like the perfect thing to sell at the new shop."

"No doubt, but I've been wondering, how will we get people in the door?"

"You can count on my brothers and me to get the place cleaned up, polished, and ready for the public. It's going to look great. I texted Nico the paint colors already. But I was thinking, there are numerous restaurants and places in town that sell baked goods and delicious food. What's going to attract people to ours so we're open by Christmas?"

"Merry, you've never experienced what six Costa men can accomplish when they put their minds to something. We're all in. Except for Paulo. He's been fairly quiet for some reason. Hope everything is okay." My younger brother is generally busy at the boxing gym where he works in New York City, but it's unusual for him to cut us out.

"That's five brothers." Merry holds out her hand with fingers splayed.

I motion as if about to give her a high five then twine my

fingers in hers, closing our palms together. Her gaze flits from our hands to my eyes. A question hovers there.

"Don't forget about Frankie," I say as if this is a perfectly normal, nothing-to-see-here moment. Nothing other than the crackling and sparking between us.

"She's about to have a baby." Merry's voice is just barely above a whisper.

"Count her in. She was repainting the walls in the nursery for the third time when she went into labor with Rafael. At least it was a natural VOC-free kind of paint. Try as we might, nothing stops that woman."

Merry breaks free then sits down at the table and leans on her elbows. "I guess I'm just worried that it's not going to work out."

I slide her hands out from under her chin and clasp them in mine again, once more trying to draw her away from the idea that this can't work. "Wasn't trust part of the pact?"

"Which pact?"

"You know which one," I hint.

She squares her shoulders, resolute. "Tommy, we can't go forward with a wedding."

"Why not?" I lean back in the chair and cross my arms, prepared for a long conversation during which I'll attempt to convince her that we should give marriage a shot.

"Because..." She swishes her mouth side to side, thinking.

"What do we have to lose? I promise I won't sneak a piece of pie unless you say I can eat it. I also won't chew all your gum or leave my backpack in the doorway."

Merry chuckles because back in college I was guilty on both counts.

"But we have the business plus pizza dough and a pie to make. And let's not forget Christmas is coming. There isn't time for a wedding or a marriage for that matter."

"All true. But thirty is in the rearview mirror, and we made a promise to each other."

"We can't marry each other just because we made a pact and some silly rules when we were twenty."

"Who says we can't? Was that one of the rules?"

Her eyes crinkle around the edges and her jaw trembles as if she fights a smile. "No, but—"

"Is there someone else? I thought you said there's no Mr. Merry."

"No, no one at all." She slouches over to the oven to check the pie.

Despite the chemistry between us, and how good it feels to talk and be with her again, my thoughts dip with doubt. Maybe she doesn't like me. I should probably shave more often. Get a haircut. If I set my ego aside, Gio can give me pointers on how not to look like a firefighter who pays more attention to working out to stay in shape and less about whether a simple outfit of jeans and a cotton shirt is suitable when dating.

This time, I rest my elbows on the table, wondering what to say to tell Merry about how I feel without scaring her away or causing her to clamp down harder on being such a responsible adult instead of the fun and carefree woman she'd always been.

I glance at the table and my eyes catch the words *Dear Santa* written across the top of a sheet of paper much like Frankie was working on with the two older kids the other day. Thinking it's innocent—maybe a project from wherever she volunteers these days because she was always involved in service work back in college—I slide the paper closer and read the note.

A zing of excitement and hope shoots through me. "Sounds like someone has been a good girl and is, in fact, looking for a mister."

In a swift and sudden movement, one hundred-something pounds of soft, fluffy robe material clobbers me. It's like a giant stuffed animal lands on me and all I want to do is snuggle, but the chair starts to pitch backward from the momentum. I try to stabilize us and stretch out the toe of my boot to catch the lip of the table for a slower descent as we drop to the floor.

Merry spawls on top of me like a flying squirrel with a pinched expression of terror as she tries to grab the paper, but I hold it out of her grasp.

"I'll give this to you if you tell me why you're resisting whatever is going on between us."

She scrambles for the note, but my long arms come in handy to keep it away from her. With my other hand, I start to tickle her so she knows I don't mean any harm.

Finally, she gives in, smiling and laughing before dropping onto my chest in an adorable heap. "Okay, okay. Fine. I'll tell you."

CHAPTER 9

MERILEE

Tommy holds his hand out to help me off the floor. No matter how many times our fingers brush or hold tight, a tingling sensation that's a combination of excitement and nervousness races through me like bubbles trying to escape a can of soda.

He picks up the chair and then sits back down. I smooth my hair, wishing I wasn't wearing this silly robe. A girl like Cassie would probably have on something cute while prancing around the kitchen, demonstrating how to knead the dough and allowing the moments shared with her crush to become more because she's not a self-conscious, self-sabotager like me.

I didn't bother changing because I told myself I can't let Tommy see how I really feel, that I care what he thinks of me, and risk experiencing rejection all over again.

This leads me to have to answer his question about what's going on between us, if only to get back my letter to Santa. I'd meant to stick it in an envelope but wanted to dig out a nice one and not a regular business mailer.

This is going to be hard to say, but I go for it, casting aside insecurities and the possibility that after this I won't be able to show my face in Hawk Ridge Hollow ever again. "The problem is that I'm not like Cassie," I blurt.

Tommy's expression puckers.

My heart sinks with the confirmation that he doesn't like me. I mean, how could he after seeing me in this getup? Why would he after he clearly preferred my roommate with the stylish clothes, outgoing personality, and the confidence of a lioness?

Remember, I'm a house mouse.

Instead of a half-smile, he wears a half-frown. The space between his eyebrows bunch with confusion or dismay, I'm not sure. "Thank goodness you're not like her. Granted, I hadn't seen Cassie much since college, but she was over the top at the wedding reception. Poor Leon."

My posture straightens slightly, surprised at that response. "What do you mean?"

Tommy's eyes narrow with what I assume is disbelief because although we never gossiped about my roommate, we'd shared plenty of secret eye rolls when in her presence. She was more than slightly—how to put this nicely?—extra, intense, a ball of frenetic energy, and always simpering for attention.

"But what about that afternoon when I got back to my dorm and you were in there, on my bed, uh...?" The words gouge their way out of what I realize now is my broken heart.

Tommy wipes his hand down his face. "I was afraid this was the problem. Yes, I was sitting on your bed because Cassie had shopping bags on the desk chair. If you recall, I was waiting for you because we'd made plans to see the play my roommate was performing in."

The memory filters back and along with it, how crushed I was to see Tommy and Cassie making out.

"I heard someone coming down the hall, checked my watch, and said, 'Ah, that must be Merry.' Cassie teased about your name, saying something dumb like, 'Merilee, Merilee, life is but a drag—'"

Even from the past, Cassie's comment pierces me. "I knew I was boring."

"If that were true, I wouldn't have spent every spare minute I had with you. Anyway, she clobbered me, much like you did when I read that note written to a certain jolly old man." Tommy arches a suggestive eyebrow.

Oh, Santa, why didn't you take the letter? I left it with a pie, for goodness' sakes!

It takes me a moment to get past the renewed embarrassment about the letter and process what else he said. "So you didn't make a move on her? She told me that you'd been flirting with her a ton and asked her on a date, but since she'd dated your roommate, she didn't want to break the bro code."

Tommy chuckles. "The bro code? That's rich coming from her. The bro code was a deal Drew Ritchie and I made. We agreed never to date someone the other guy had already been with. He'd gone on a date with Cassie freshman year and mentioned that it was about as fun as having a mosquito in your ear."

I recall Drew's southern sayings and ask how he's doing these days.

"Returned to the family ranch in Texas and has a family of his own. He's well. Anyway, as you know, I'm a man of my word and don't break an agreement."

He captures my gaze in his. It's intense with a side of smolder. The hum under my skin isn't sure how to settle. Do I believe Tommy who has never done anything (other than that alleged incident) to give me a reason not to trust him? Or Cassie who had a different boyfriend every month and brought more drama to our dorm than everyone else combined? Not to mention how she made every effort to make me feel about the size of a house mouse.

"So you really didn't like Cassie?"

"I only went to her wedding because I secretly hoped you'd

be there and figured I might see some other old friends from college. But no, I didn't like her that way. Let's see. Where to start? The overwhelming amount of perfume she wore would cause me a major flare-up now. The fixation on her attire was tiresome—how many times did she make us late because she needed to ask you what you thought of her outfit then changed it multiple times before we left the dorm? Oh, and the incessant whispering with whoever she was with and darty eye movements in my direction whenever I came by with a guy friend or when I met up with you. It always made me feel self-conscious."

"I thought you, er, guys, like girly girls like that."

Tommy tugs on the hem of my robe. "Girly girls? Like ones who wear fluffy robes in the softest shade of pink?"

Marriage pact or not, we made an agreement, a pact, to be honest with each other. As hard as this is, if I can't talk to him about how I feel, there's no hope Santa will bring me a guy for Christmas...or ever.

"I mean like girls who know how to do things like, um, flirt with guys." I squeeze my eyes shut, terrified of his response.

He gets up from the chair. Nervous excitement zips through me at the thought of him grabbing the robe's tie around my waist again and drawing me close, but he lifts the cloth over the pizza dough and takes a peek. "It's obtaining blob status." Laughter fills his lips when he looks up at me.

I fight a grin because this man is too tempting for his own good. "I thought that word is off-limits?"

"I was evening out the playing field." Now, flips on the oven light and inspects the pie. "Looks irresistible."

The sweet and buttery berry scent fills the room and gives me confidence because I may not be a flirt, but I do know how to bake. Perhaps I can telegraph some of my know-how into being more of a temptation.

"You too." I look from my left to my right, not sure who said that. Oh, wait. It was me because Tommy Costa is too alluring for my own good.

The corner of his mouth lifts into the smirkiest of smirks. "You think I'm also irresistible, Merry? Good. Because to finish what I was saying before, I don't like girls like Cassie who wear a lot of lipstick. It makes them harder to kiss."

My jaw trembles when I say, "But you did kiss her."

Tommy shakes his head. "Looking back now, I can see why you thought it looked like we were kissing. Wish I'd realized it then. I figured you knew me better than that. If you don't believe me, would you like me to demonstrate what happened between us?"

I laugh, suddenly feeling light with relief. "You really didn't kiss her?"

"I'd just as soon smooch the blob."

I cringe. "Cooties."

"Good point."

"And points deducted because that word is off-limits."

He flashes his half-smile. "Fair enough. But the truth is you're adorable. The problem is you don't even realize it."

I whimper a little because something in me resists giving in to accepting his sweet words.

"And I like girls like you. Girls who flirt." Tommy winks.

"Tommy, I do not know how to flirt."

He places his hands on my arms "What have we been doing all day? What did we do back in college?"

I open and close my mouth, stammering. "Nadine says I'm garlic bread for guys."

"Good thing I love garlic bread. If I didn't know better, I'd argue that you minored in the fine art of flirting. Got top marks by my account."

"Tommy—"

"What's it going to take to prove to you that nothing went on between Cassie and me? That I made the pact to marry you by the time we turned thirty because I thought we had two more years at college together, during which I intended to propose. The pact said we'd get married *by* thirty, not *at* thirty. I thought the whole thing was just part of our slow burn romance." He hangs his head. "Then you stopped replying to my texts and we stopped hanging out, leaving me to believe you regretted it. When you left, I thought I was the one who got burned, but I realized you were probably preoccupied with your grandmother since she was sick."

I nod at everything he says because he's right. "I'm sorry for not communicating better. I was afraid you chose Cassie over me."

"Never. It wasn't even a consideration. You're adorable, irresistible, and beautiful. Merry, I chose you...I still do."

Cassie's voice of criticism inside me refutes everything Tommy just said in much the same way Nadine tossed what Nan identified as backhanded insults my way. "I don't know why you'd still want to marry me." Moreover, why am I listening to Cassie or Nadine rather than my grandmother or Tommy?

He gently taps my temple. "Are you still listening to whatever garbage Cassie told you or are you going to listen to me? Believe me?"

"It's like you read my mind."

He winks and pinches my robe before giving it a little shake. "You wear your emotions on your fuzzy sleeve, Merry."

I hover in the clouds, not sure whether I'm about to go up or land hard on my butt. "But when I walked into the dorm room, it looked like you guys were—" I shake my head. "It's burned there like a page in an anti-scrapbook. Something I don't want to remember but can't forget. The truth is, it crushed me."

Tommy's eyes soften and he shifts closer to me. "This is how it went."

With him so close, my heart skips a beat, and a little shake rolls from my head to my toes.

However, instead of placing his lips on mine, Tommy rubs his face against my neck, snuffing like a dog looking for a hidden bone. I giggle like he's tickling me again.

When he straightens, he says, "That was the extent of my interaction with Cassie. If you didn't gather, it was entirely unpleasant."

"That wasn't horrible, but you're right. It was not a kiss."

"Not by a long shot."

"I walked in on Cassie making out with guys enough times to know she had some experience in that department, so why didn't she go for your mouth, at least?"

"The difference was, I didn't want to kiss her back. I was actively trying to get her off me."

"But why'd she do that? Especially if she knew I kind of, could've possibly, um, that I liked you."

Tommy makes a "Gotcha" gesture because I just admitted that I had a crush on him. "Because she's Cassie. The kind of girl who tears others down to build herself up. As the oldest and with five brothers and a sister I wanted to protect, I learned a thing or two about different types of people."

I droop as Cassie's backhanded comments and insults return, wondering why she'd targeted me.

Tommy grips my arms, tethering me to this moment and not the past.

"Yes, you saw us on your bed. Yes, she pressed herself against me. Yes, she licked me."

"Ew." I stick out my tongue.

"I omitted that part during my demonstration because I didn't want to gross you out."

"Thanks for sparing me. Why didn't Cassie just go for it with you?"

"Maybe she wasn't as confident as she made herself out to be. Perhaps she saw a boat load of confidence in you and felt inadequate so she tried to make up for that by trying to make you feel teeny tiny. Probably because I was trying to get her off me without using a heavy hand," Tommy says, referring to my comment about how he kneaded the dough.

My jaw drops open. "Do you think she saw the pact? You'd left the notebook on my desk after we'd studied one night. She probably looked through it and saw what we'd written." What she did still stings, but I feel bad for her if she thought she had to hurt me to feel better about herself.

"Likely theory. What matters is that I did not like Cassie and I didn't kiss her."

Finally understanding, I let out a long breath, relieved that I'd had it wrong.

"So you believe me? I didn't kiss Cassie, and she didn't kiss me?" Tommy asks.

I nod as a smirk slides across my face. "Even so, that's not how you kiss. I'm not the most experienced in that department, but licking like that usually isn't involved."

With a facetious smile, Tommy says, "It's not? In that case, would you care to demonstrate how a kiss is done? After all, you were really good at helping me learn how to knead the pizza dough."

I playfully whack him with the dishtowel.

His espresso brown eyes on mine wake me up to the fact that he's not joking. Closing the space between us, Tommy plants his hands on my waist.

Flutters work their way outward from my stomach as our gazes hold and the moment lengthens.

"You're not kidding, are you?" My voice is almost a whisper.

"No, the kiss that I've been waiting to have for over ten years, the one we never got to share, will clear your record for breaking the blob law."

"But you're the one on probation."

"Two wrongs make a right?" he asks.

I bite my lip to steady my trembling jaw as realization

dawns. I'm so afraid of sealing things between Tommy and me because what if he rejects me? It would be like dashing all my hopes and dreams.

Then again, with him, I'm making the one about opening my own bakery come true. Can I give in and let what we built between us and then put on hold all this time finally happen?

I lift onto my toes and plant my lips softly on Tommy's. It's a tame kiss. A tease. Something to make him want more because maybe I do know how to flirt after all—at least that's how it works when I've given out samples of my pie.

Tommy's eyes remained closed, telling me he does indeed want more. The throbbing in my chest and the smile on my face tells me that I do too.

CHAPTER 10

TOMMY

*M*erry's lips press against mine so softly, it was like a whisper, a suggestion, a possibility of something wonderful to come.

In my mind, I see a blue sky, fluffy clouds, and a woman so innocently sweet that she should be illegal.

That one tease of a kiss makes me want more, makes me wonder what's over the horizon, beyond the simplicity of two lips merely pressing together. I lean closer.

My eyes remain closed because I don't want the adventure to be over. I want to keep going. I want Merry.

I inhale, imprinting the way we came together, even briefly, into my mind like a full sensory photograph.

Soft. Sweet. The scent of apples. A twinkling between us.

I'm about to blink open my eyes when her hands grip my shoulders, drawing me lower, and her mouth joins mine again. My palms find her jawline and I return the kiss. The flare that rises inside me could produce a five-alarm fire. The kiss deepens as blazes of light and the roaring of my pulse sounds in my ears.

Our hands remain anchored, yet it's all mouth, all motion.

Our breathing moves together like we're both nearing the same destination, the same conclusion.

I love this woman. I made the marriage pact because I meant it as much then as now. I want a future with her.

My body heats with the possibility that I can experience her soft lips on mine, her fingers threading into my hair, her heart pounding, and cheeks shining every day, any time, always.

A beeping sound enters my awareness. I travel back to where I am in space and time—Merry's kitchen. The oven. Pie.

She drops onto her heels as we both open our eyes, gazes searching. My entire being swells with affection, warmth, and a desire to do this again and again 'til death do we part.

Her gaze flickers and she places her hand on my chest and turns to the oven without a word...or a smile.

A splash of water douses the flame inside, or perhaps I'm imagining things.

Surely, the kiss confirmed how we feel about each other. If the first kiss was a sparkler, a soft brush of lips, this one was fireworks. Right?

Although, now it's as if the tension from earlier returns, leaving me uncertain about where we stand, so I lower into the chair.

Unlike when we were back in college, I'm not going to be King Doofus and ignore or deny how I feel about Merry.

She sets the pie on a cooling rack and moves swiftly around the kitchen before presenting me with the risen pizza dough.

"Poke it, and see how it bounces back." She demonstrates then goes on to talk about different dough methods—slow versus rapid proofing times, various fermentation styles, options for a room temperature rise or refrigeration, and suggestions I might want to try at the pizza shop.

Quite frankly, it's overwhelming when all I want to do is linger in the kiss.

I'm about to reach my arm around her, to hang onto her and

onto the moment we shared when she zips across the kitchen and grabs a flat, wooden tool she identifies as a pizza peel.

"Ready to toss?" she asks with a tremulous smile.

Did she just toss out the kiss? Move on so quick? Forget the intensity we so recently shared?

I need a few minutes to think about how I'm going to ask these questions so I follow her instructions on how to toss the dough into a round disk.

True to my Italian heritage, I manage not to get the dough stuck on the ceiling nor does it flop to the floor. In the end, it's more of an oval shape like the classic margarita pizzas in the old country.

"Nice job," Merry says.

"Is my reward a piece of pie?" Another kiss?

"Ha ha. That's for tomorrow. We have a lot of work to do."

"So you're dangling a carrot?" Is that what the kiss was too?

"A sweet, buttery carrot."

"My favorite kind."

She laughs again, making me wonder if I was just being insecure a few minutes ago and I misread her body language. Time to find out.

"In that case, how about another kiss?" My voice is rough and filled with desire.

She pauses a beat.

My pulse jumps.

Merry's smile dims. "I don't know if that's a good idea."

My heart stops.

"I was just thinking, with our business together, with all the pressure and stress that's sure to come, we probably shouldn't get romantically involved. Like how corporations have human resource policies that forbid romantic involvement between employees."

Frankie jokes that I'm like a human furnace, but I go cold, frigid. "But it's just us. We can make it work. Merry, I—"

She faces me and smooths her palm along my jawline. "Tommy, I care a lot about you, but I don't want to risk our friendship and business if there are things we don't agree on. Going further than that and becoming romantically involved could cause problems."

"I care a lot about you too. See? We agree."

"I'm talking more about the business side of things. We have a lot at stake, opening this place. There's so much to do. At first, we're going to be putting in long hours, will have to make a lot of decisions, and work really hard."

"But we'll be doing it together."

"And I want us to stay that way. I don't want differences or stress to tear us apart."

I take a deep breath, preparing to point out the obvious. "The only difference is that we disagree on how to handle this. We can see where things go with us, heck, even get married as well as run a pizza and pie shop together."

"I'm afraid it could all fall apart."

I brush my hand over my mouth. "Was the kiss not—?"

She throws her arms around me then tips her head up and meets my eyes. "Tommy, the kiss was years of my fantasies coming true. It was perfect. It was even better than I imagined."

"Then what's wrong? What changed?" Confusion and, I'll admit, hurt causes me to stagger backward.

"We're no longer college kids where our biggest worry is passing an exam and deciding where we're going to go to celebrate afterward. The shop is a big deal, the culmination of a dream I had. Sure, it's not exactly how I expected it to go, but—"

"Maybe it'll be even better."

"I'm hoping that's the case, but if you and I move forward with a relationship or the marriage pact, we could ruin it all."

"Or we could *not* ruin it. That's an option too much like all the choices you gave me for the pizza dough." A stubborn refusal to prevent a repeat of what happened in college, where we let our obvious affection for each other disappear, threatens to take over.

"Tommy, we can't have both the marriage pact and the business pact. We can't afford both." Her tone contains finality, resolve.

She mentioned she's financially broke, but this breaks me up inside.

"Let's see what happens," I say, almost pleading because I lost Merry once and won't easily give into defeat.

Her sky-blue eyes blink slowly as if she's contemplating. Then she turns her head to the side and takes a spoon out of a drawer.

Inspiration shoves my stubbornness out of the way. I'm going to prove to her that she can have her pie and eat it too. But like waiting for the pizza dough to rise, I'll have to be patient.

"I'll put some toppings on the pizza and bake it for tomorrow to eat after we get started cleaning the shop. We'll have our first pizza and pie lunch."

Feeling dismissed, I take it that's my cue to leave and shove my arms in my jacket. "Thanks for the dough lesson...and the kiss." Part of me wants to be gloomy, but when I say the last part an unbidden grin rises to my lips.

Tension stretches between us. Merry mentioned dough can rise quickly or can be left longer to proof. Once more, I remind myself to be patient.

"See you in the morning," she says.

"Bright and early. Remember, I'll pick you up because your car is at the shop."

Her shoulders drop slightly. "Forgot about that. Thanks again."

"Thought so and don't mention it. It's what business partners, and boyfriends, do."

"Tommy..."

"Merry..." I reply with a smile and a yawn, lifting my arms over my head, and the hem of my shirt comes with it.

Her expression softens and turns dreamy once more. Maybe we're both tired.

I could kiss her again right now but will respect her boundaries. They're about as strong as pie dough, and I cannot wait to prove to her that the sweetness between us can work.

"Oh, one more thing," she says as if not wanting me to leave despite her insistence that we do not mix business and pleasure. "About the note to Santa, since I showed it to you, am I clear of the charges for breaking the rules and mentioning the you-know-what?"

"Absolved." But that reminds me that she wants a guy, a relationship.

I'll see to it that Santa delivers her gift by Christmas.

The next morning, snow mounds along the sides of the street. Merry is ready to work when I pick her up. With her hair in a ponytail, she wears a pair of paint-splattered overalls and a T-shirt from a college event that pitted early birds against night owls. Her shirt is yellow with a badger on it wearing a blue hat, our school's mascot. She looks as adorable now as she did then.

"Nice T-shirt."

"Nice face," she replies.

Her's goes pink. "I meant nice place. This is a nice place you have here, Mr. Costa." She gestures around the distinctly *not* nice pizza shop.

Seeing it again, in the light of day and without the rosy lenses of hope, opportunity, and smitten-with-Merry goggles, we really do have a lot of work ahead of us.

Over the next half hour, the troops arrive—Nico first, who's on trash removal duty.

"What are Ma and Pop doing?" I ask him.

"They're at home, enjoying being snowed in and cooking up a storm. Prepare yourselves for a major meal tonight," Nico says.

"Looking forward to it. Merry brought us pizza and pie for lunch." Standing next to me, I start to sling my arm over her shoulder and then pull back, remembering her new rule. Then again, it's not a written amendment to the pact. But for now, I'd better not push my luck.

"Ah, and they want the Future Mrs. Costa to join us." Nico wears a smirk as if he knows that this isn't a normal engagement.

A blush rises to her cheeks and she stammers, "Me?"

"You got it, sis," Nico says and does sling his arm around her. "There are probably a few things you should know about my older brother." He leans in as if about to expose my secrets.

What are they? I'm not sure, but he'll make up something.

Wanting to spare her and myself further embarrassment, I peel his arm off. "Trash duty."

"Alright. Alright. But we'll chat later." My baby brother winks at Merry.

"Whatever he says, don't listen to him."

"Oh, come on. I was going to tell her that you're the most upstanding, caring, and smelly member of this family."

"Trash," I growl.

Merry laughs and says, "Where were we?"

The word *we* gives me hope and strengthens my resolve to make her the Future Mrs. Costa.

Her blue-eyed gaze searches mine before I answer her question.

I'd like to pick up where we left off last night after the kiss. Instead, I say, "Making a plan of attack to get this place cleaned up, fixed up, and ready to open."

"Right. Thankfully, I already did a lot of the research for how to run a business, but now it's a matter of implementing it before Christmas."

"When I talked to my siblings about doing this for our family and our parents, we decided that I'll run the place. Frankie is making the menu—"

As if on cue, Frankie waddles through the front door, belly leading the way, and stomps off her boots on the mat. She holds out a piece of paper. "The official menu."

"That was fast." I browse the list of appetizers, salads, and pizza combinations.

"I've had some cravings." Frankie opens her arms. "Future Mrs. Costa—"

The pink in Merry's cheeks darkens at the second mention of her being the Future Mrs. Costa.

Completely out of character, Frankie pulls Merry into a hug. Having six brothers didn't exactly make her the touchy-feely type. Then again, motherhood probably changed that. "I've always wanted a sister."

My eyes bulge.

Merry whispers, "Not counting Nadine, me too."

Interesting that she'd make that comment considering the separation of business and pleasure she instated.

The two chat for a few minutes then we give Frankie a tour.

"Up here is the front-of-house dining area. We won't do table service, counter orders only, but guests can eat in or dine out," I explain, picturing the place full of people.

"I love the huge front windows with the view of town and the mountains in the background," Frankie says approvingly.

"Over here is the order counter, drink dispensers, warm beverage station, and pick-up area."

Merry adds, "This display case down here will be for the pies and these shelves up top are for selling pizza by the slice."

I point out the woodfired pizza oven in the corner behind the counter. "I'll be inspecting that tomorrow."

"And here's the supply closet, bathroom, office, and then we'll head to the kitchen with several stainless steel prep tables, walk-in fridge, regular ovens, stove and grill, and the salad preparation unit," Merry says.

When we enter, I point to a metal contraption from the last century. "And of course, the sinks and dishwashing machine."

"Which doesn't work," Nico hollers from the front.

"We'll fix it," I holler back.

"Do you really think you'll have enough room back here for pie baking and pizza making?" Frankie's eyebrows ripple with concern. "It'll be cozy."

I lift and lower mine, liking the sound of that.

Merry's forehead furrows. "I've given it some thought, and I'll have baker's hours, meaning I'll come in early and do my work then stay through the morning. I'll have to hire someone to take over for the afternoon, but by then all the baking will be done."

"Good plan. I trust you'll make it work. Pizza and pie. An unusual but perfect combination," Frankie says. "If I come up with any crossover menu items, you'll be the first to know. I have to admit, I cannot wait to see my big brother in action."

"I can handle a little heat in the kitchen."

My sister smirks at the two of us. "No doubt."

Bruno and Luca arrive next. We make introductions.

Bruno obnoxiously corrects, "I go by Bryan."

I roll my eyes. He must think it sounds more professional in the business world or something. "Whatever, Bruno. He's our numbers guy and will keep the books. Can do yours too, if you'd like," I offer to Merry.

My brother scowls at me for volunteering him, but he knows that as the oldest, what I say goes. "First order of business, what are we going to call this place if not Hawk Ridge Hollow Pizza?"

Merry stammers.

"How about Hawk Ridge Hollow Pizza and Pie."

"It's a mouthful," she says.

"Exactly," I add but sense she doesn't like the name. "How

about that for now unless we come up with something a bit more catchy? It'll be a bit before we get signage."

She nods as if overwhelmed. My family can do that.

"This bearded bandit is Luca who'll tackle inventory."

He grunts.

Gio, the fourth in line rolls up in a Porsche. "Meet Giovanni, who looks far too stylish today. He's is our PR man. He'll get the word out. For now, he's going to be doing the dirty work."

"Isn't there a sixth brother?" Merry asks.

I look around as if hearing crickets. "Who's missing? Oh, right. Paulo."

"He's been busy," Nico says carefully like he knows something I don't.

I grunt, putting off my irritation at his absence until later when I'll call him and share a few choice words. Most of them are in Italian. I won't let our parents overhear or else I'll get a scolding. Yes, even though I'm in my mid-thirties.

I clap my hands together. "*Famiglia*, between now and lunch, we're going to clean this place until it gleams. Then, this afternoon, we're going to paint and construct a few shelves and other items. Nico already hauled out most of the trash so we have a blank template. Any questions, ask Merry or me. Okay, go."

Bruno and Luca head to the kitchen, Gio takes the front, and Nico tackles the area behind the counter.

"It's great that your brothers are all chipping in, but do you really think we can do all of this in one day?"

"Future Mrs. Costa, you have yet to see this family in action."

A sad expression drifts across Merry's face and then just as quickly disappears. "Tommy, remember what I said last night?"

"I remember what I read last night." I hope my eyes twinkle like Santa's when I glance at Merry knowingly. Before she can protest about my seeing her letter, I say, "As for you and me, we have to clean the office and bathroom, then what?"

"We have branding to figure out and orders to make—everything from soup to nuts, straws to napkins, and food. Um, you know about my savings situation, but I feel like I should ask how are you planning to afford this? I assume you didn't take out a loan between yesterday and today. It'll be a lot of cash up front, especially for you with wholesale food orders and things like that."

"I too have savings and plan on getting as much of the food and other services locally. Farm to table style."

"So you're not going with the classic, greasy pizza like from Signori Pepperoni's?"

"While I cannot deny that I love myself a good greasy slice from time to time, check out Frankie's menu." I show her the sample my sister brought by.

She browses the pizzas listed, covered with toppings like fresh mozzarella, prosciutto, sundried tomatoes, and olives.

"My mouth is watering," Merry says. "This looks great. The perfect complement to my pies ranging from the standard apple to the more unusual apple bacon." She lowers her voice to a whisper. "My favorite."

"Sounds delicious." I bump her with my hip. "See? We already make a great team."

Her smile flickers with interest then she casts her gaze away. "We do work well together, but we can't mess up our friendship."

"I thought it was the business relationship you were concerned about?"

Merry's expression darkens as she looks out the window and into the distance. She shakes her head slowly. "Tommy, we just can't."

My chest suddenly feels dark, hollow, cave-like—similar to the place where I spent last year after I left the fire department. I'm smart enough to know Merry can't prevent me from returning to that level of desolation. However, her smile, laughter, and our time together illuminate all the shadows that now tell me to crawl back inside.

I let out a sigh, preparing myself to talk to her about whatever is going on between us. However, when I follow her gaze, I spot a CoffeeHut van parked outside on the street.

CHAPTER 11

MERILEE

Torn between wanting to rush down the street to the local church and tie the knot with Tommy right this second and knowing I ought to be a responsible business-owning adult, focused on building (and protecting) her pie empire, I freeze, immobile, and unable to do anything after I spot a potential enemy.

I'd like to rush outside to where the CoffeeHut van idles like a spy mobile casing the joint. It's black with a brown coffee cup on the side and the white logo on the two front doors. Hands on hips, I'd signal for the driver to roll down the window and tell him to get lost.

Instead, I sit quietly beside Tommy. He gives off the kind of warmth that I'd like to curl up beside on a cold winter's night.

We're great as friends but would be even better together. I can't let that happen because if it didn't work out, how would we manage this shop together? It would all fall apart and I can't afford that. Enough people in this town have seen me taking odd jobs, coming and going, and this time, I have to succeed. I refuse to be seen as a failure again.

"What do you suppose the CoffeeHut van is doing here?" he asks.

My stormy thoughts interrupted, I say, "Who? Oh, right, maybe they're looking for pizza and pie."

"We're not open yet."

"Do you think Tobias Marley sent him to put some pressure on us?"

"Nah. We gave him the security deposit plus the first and last months' rent, which should cover his taxes. I'm guessing he doesn't want us to fail and be out a tenant, hence the Christmas deadline."

"Then why do you think the CoffeeHut van is here?" I ask.

Tommy gets to his feet, a formidable Italian man who I wouldn't want to meet in a dark alley behind a pizza place or in front of it for that matter—we used to watch all the mob movies and shows together in college.

A slim guy with a wispy mustache and pale skin exits the van. He surveys the exterior of the building before peering through the glass door and then stepping inside. "Hello, hello. Looks like you guys are getting this place whipped into shape. Lookin' good. Lookin' good. Are you from Demos-R-Us or the Demolition Dream Team? I have to know who to write a check to."

Tommy tilts his head to one side. "What was that?"

The man juts out his hand for Tommy to shake. "I'm Rob Lasker from CoffeeHut."

"Can we help you?" Tommy asks.

"I've been in talks with the building owner and we're on schedule to rent it out for the latest CoffeeHut installment. Unfortunately, there was a little delay so we won't be able to get in until after the new year. Bummer to miss the Christmas rush. However, glad to see Marley got someone in here to fix up this dump. Then we can just slap up a sign and get the coffee flowing." He chortles, sending a gust of gross coffee breath my way.

I step forward, time to adult up because I'm not letting Coffee Breath waltz in here like he owns the place. "Hi, I'm Merilee Ketchum and I bake pies. This is Tommy Costa and he's doing pizzas. It's a unique concept, but it's going to sell like hot...pies. We co-own this business and already signed a rental agreement with Tobias Marley. There must be a mistake or a misunderstanding."

"Is that so?" Coffee Breath Lasker's upper lip twitches. His eyes rake over me then he takes my hand in his. "The pleasure is mine, Miss Ketchum. You said you signed a lease? Well, we can fix that."

My eyebrows pinch together. "What do you mean?"

"Miss Ketchum, I'm backed by a multi-million dollar corporation. This is a prime location with CoffeeHut written all over it. This Podunk town is ripe for the taking. How much can I offer you to walk away?"

"Walk away?" I repeat, unsure if he's offering a payoff.

"Yep. Buh-bye. *Adios*. What do you Italians say? *Ciao*?" Rob Lasker flashes a condescending smile to the man towering over him.

Tommy scowls.

I catch his gaze and then shake my head slowly and definitively. "I'm not walking away."

"Me neither," Tommy says, voice lethal.

Frowning, Coffee Breath paces a short circle around the dining room and stops in front of me. "Maybe not willingly." I'm not sure if the words are an incomplete thought or a threat.

Nico pokes his head out of the kitchen's double swinging doors. "Future Mrs. Costa, I'm wondering if you want me to keep these old bus bins? They're in decent shape."

"Yes, please. That would be great. Thank you, Nico."

For the first time since Coffee Breath appeared, Tommy's features soften.

"Future Mrs. Costa?" Coffee Breath asks with a narrow-eyed

sneer. "Does that mean you're not married yet but are going into business together? Tsk. Tsk. You know that there's a ninety-nine percent failure rate when mixing business with pleasure."

My stomach churns because that's exactly what I'm afraid of.

"You'd know that, wouldn't you?" Tommy mutters, full-on stone-faced again.

"Here's my business card for when you change your mind. I expect CoffeeHut will be opening on schedule in the new year." He sweeps out the door before I can say another word.

Tommy and I stand there in stunned silence while the van pulls away.

"What just happened? Did you know him?" I ask.

He tears up the business card and tosses it in the trash. "No, but I've come across guys like him. Reeks of arrogance and greed. He doesn't care about coffee or Hawk Ridge Hollow. Just wants to open another cookie-cutter coffee shop so he can rip people off and make more money."

"Speaking of cookies, I have to meet with Mrs. Cringle. In addition to doing a baked goods swap, she asked me to work a stall at the church's Christmas bazaar this weekend as well as sell some pies at the welcome center on the edge of town. I figured it would be a good jumpstart to get the word out about our place. But do you think Coffee Breath is going to try to—?"

Tommy interrupts with a deep belly laugh. "Coffee Breath?"

I wave my hand in front of my face. "I've never tried CoffeeHut beverages, but if they make their customer's breath smell like Rob Lasker's, they ought to give out free mouthwash."

Tommy slings his arm around my shoulder.

I welcome the weight, the steadiness, and familiarity of it against the tide of uncertainty that just swept through here.

"Don't worry about Coffee Breath. He just wants to undermine us."

I close my eyes, wanting to lean into Tommy and find assurance that everything is going to work out. But I have to stay strong and resist my heart's desire. I shrug out from his embrace.

Tommy blinks slowly as if remembering my rule.

"Do you think what he said about business partnerships failing was true?"

Tommy exhales sharply. "If Cassie weren't already married, I'd introduce them. They'd be the perfect match." He storms into the kitchen, muttering something harsh in Italian under his breath.

All I can think about is Coffee Breath's comment about couples in business failing, making me believe I made the right decision to build a no-dating wall between Tommy and me.

But if that's the case, why is my stomach queasy and my chest fluttering with anxiety? If my intuition knows something I don't, I'd prefer it not make me feel like I just gobbled down a bowl of pure sugar, followed it with a jug of honey, and then downed some maple syrup just to be sure my pulse goes sufficiently haywire and prompts an unpleasant amount of nervous sweat. Perhaps it could have the taste of a tart apple or a sour lemon. That would be better.

Still, I'm not sure how to identify what I feel.

No, that's not true. I want Tommy, but that step leads to uncharted and dangerous territory because it could mean losing so much...and I've already lost everyone I love.

From the dining room, Italian words rise and fall. Even though I know all of twelve phrases with thanks to Tommy back in college, I get the sense he relayed the interaction with Coffee Breath to his brothers.

The usually boisterous and talkative Costas are relatively subdued while we eat pizza and pie for lunch. I take a few notes for the pizza crust to relay to Tommy. The pie is good, but nothing tastes right. It's like I tossed my appetite in the trash. Why do I feel so off today? Something is out of alignment—the whisper of Nan's voice tells me it's my mind and heart. But I ignore it.

The rest of the afternoon is like a home-improvement show montage featured on my favorite HLTV show, Designed to Last.

Cobwebs and dust disappear, replaced with fresh paint, clear windows, and a polished floor. It could definitely stand to be refinished, but between it and one of the exposed brick walls, it lends a rustic feel that could work really well with the branding ideas I'm developing—a country yet contemporary blend of dinner and dessert, flavorful combinations, and an irresistible dude. I mean dough. I totally meant dough.

The idea of being the Future Mrs. Costa is like my Christmas dream come true, but it can't be with Tommy. There's too much at stake.

By the end of the day, the shop looks like it underwent a complete transformation like on the aforementioned home improvement show. Everything is spotlessly clean, scrubbed, and polished. The space smells like paint, but not for long because as soon as we get the ovens fired up there will be a combination of doughs—sweet and savory.

After the Costa clan heads over to Tommy's for dinner, he and I do a quick walk-through before we lock up. I make a list of things we need to purchase including an ice scoop, floor mats, and a couple of oven thermometers.

"I have a surprise for you." Tommy's half-smile catches me in the half-light of the fading day.

The name *Future Mrs. Costa* fluttered into my mind towing a rainbow and a pot of golden love. I push hard against a potential smile.

"Hey, don't frown. It's not particularly romantic if that's what you're worried about."

I snort because for a split second, that was exactly what I was worried about.

"I had the plumber come by. Turned out the you-know-what in the sink was indeed pizza dough left to rise."

"Why didn't it decompose?"

"The relative moisture in the pipes fed the yeast. More like a beast. See, I was paying attention during your science lesson."

I laugh.

"Don't worry. It's all gone. Anyway, forget opening by Christmas. If we continue at this pace, we'll be ready to serve by December first," he says.

I gasp. "That's in two days."

"Tomorrow, we'll put in our orders."

"And I'll be baking a couple dozen pies for the church's Christmas bazaar."

"Can you make it a couple dozen and one? I asked my brothers to save a slice for Ma and Pop to share, but they wolfed it down."

"I'll make two extra."

"Okay, but only if you come to dinner tonight." The corner of Tommy's lips lift with a smirk.

"I have a lot to do. I should probably head home. We have another full day tomorrow, and I have to get baking those pies."

Tommy links his pinky around mine. "Future Mrs. Costa or not, you do not want to miss my mom's meatballs and sauce."

"I don't think it's a good idea."

"My parents would disagree. They really liked you."

"We only met for a few minutes."

"My brothers have been keeping them filled in on how you're a hard worker, have a good sense of humor, and an adorable smile."

"*They've* been talking about me or—?"

Tommy holds up his hands as if guilty. "Alright. It was me. I told my parents those things."

"They think we're getting married. I can't lie." I shake my head slowly.

Just then headlights sweep across the front windows. I shield my eyes.

Tobias Marley stumps up the stairs and throws open the door. "I hear some shenanigans are going on. What's this about you two getting married? Don't you know that there's a ninety-nine percent failure rate when mixing business with pleasure?"

Tommy's arms cross in front of his broad chest. "Where'd you hear that?"

I give the air a short little punch and mutter, "Coffee Breath."

"What's that, miss? Or should I say the Future Mrs. Costa? Listen, I need this place to stay occupied under the order of the town. Should it go vacant again, I'm in hot water."

"Sir, with all due respect, we had a visit earlier from a CoffeeHut representative who was under the impression that you're renting the space to him in January. Considering we already paid you and are under contract, can you please explain what's happening?" Tommy's voice goes deep, all business.

Mr. Marley coughs awkwardly as if he has a hairball or we caught him in a fib. "That was a misunderstanding. However, in addition to being fully operational by Christmas—"

Tommy interrupts. "Please, have a look around. You can see we already made significant progress."

Mr. Marley turns in a slow circle and his eyes broaden with surprise then turn droopy and sad. "So you did. How'd you pull this off? Hire a small army?"

"No, my family gave us a hand."

Marley nods slowly, his expression no longer sharp, accusatory. "I remember Judy working here like it was yesterday."

"This place was once the talk of the town," I say, fondly recalling visits with Gramps.

"That it was." As if pulling himself out of reverie or getting a glimpse of Christmas past, Mr. Marley plants his hands on our shoulders and says, "Merilee, Tommy, if you're going into business together, I must also insist you both be in a committed relationship."

"But—" I'm about to object because I expected him to forbid we have any romantic involvement given the comment earlier about the ninety-nine percent failure rate.

"Sir, did we hear you correctly?" Tommy asks.

He clasps his hands over his belly. "I don't know what got into me. My apologies. I may not look like it, but I'm a family man. This was once a family-run business owned by my late wife's family. In fact, I was just recalling that we met right over there." He points to the table by the window. "She brought me a shaker of parmesan cheese." The corner of his lips quiver with sadness.

"That's so sweet," I say then whisper, "Thank you, Mrs. Marley." I have a feeling she miraculously stepped in, softened his heart, and reminded her husband what's important.

"My Judy was a good woman. Made me a good man. Sometimes it's easier to forget, but that doesn't make it better. Anyway, I can't force you two to get hitched or anything, but if you're considering it, don't hesitate. Run to the church and say *I do*."

Tommy and I smile as if not sure what to make of his about-face and the comment.

Mr. Marley's expression remains serious.

"Sir, I'm working on it," Tommy says with a wink.

I just don't know how we can make a relationship and a business work.

Mr. Marley softens further and offers us use of the office space on the second floor before he leaves.

I turn to Tommy and say, "Yeah, I could really use a meatball right now."

I could also watch Tommy roll up his sleeves, yawn with his

arms over his head, revealing a peek of his perfect abs, or have his lips on mine in a sugar and spice kiss again. But I can't have everything I want, now can I?

CHAPTER 12

TOMMY

No one can argue that what Merry, my brothers, and I accomplished at the shop in a single day is nothing short of impressive. Of course, there are numerous tasks to complete as well as the not-insignificant issue of actually getting the place ready for the public.

However, when I got home after the long day, I had one of those cartoon eye bulge moments. My parents decorated the house from top to bottom for Christmas.

When I left this morning, there wasn't a tree, garland, fifteen stockings, or colorful lights. The additional stockings are for Frankie's family and one for Merry. Plus, angels with trumpets glow in the windows, red bows and baubles seem to duplicate themselves as I walk from room to room, and a wreath the size of a jumbo pizza hangs on the door.

Not only that but they cooked a meal that's sure to get Merry to agree to our union if only for the food benefits. We have meatballs as promised, garlic bread, creamy polenta with parmesan cheese, lemon asparagus risotto, and even lasagna. The dessert is frozen tiramisu from the market. Typically an Italian favorite with delicate sponge cake ladyfingers dipped in coffee with a sweet, creamy filling, and sprinkled with cocoa, my family agrees it's not the best they've ever had. Unfortunately, neither Ma nor Pop are particularly gifted in baking.

However, around a mouthful, Merry blurts, "Tiramisu, where have you been all my life?"

Everyone chuckles and she turns as red as Ma's marinara.

Everyone has an opinion on how it could've been better. I'll admit, even I wax poetic about how much I love a good tiramisu.

All the while, it's the strangest thing. Ma doesn't leave Merry's side, encouraging her to eat more, and asking about the pies she bakes. Typically, when any of us bring girls home, our mother turns up her nose and asks pointed questions as if to see if they're good enough for her precious sons. Yes, all while insisting we get hitched. Go figure. Instead of the shrewd and somewhat critical woman I expect her to be, she instantly warms to Merry. To my surprise, she even offers to help her at the bazaar this weekend.

Later, when I ask what she thinks of Merry, my mother says, *"What's not to like?"*

Exactly.

I don't have the heart to tell my mother that Merry is cautiously skeptical about us being together, but I'm working on changing that along with perfecting the pizza dough.

The next day, I don't see much of either of them as they bake pies for the church's Christmas bazaar together at Merry's house.

Unfortunately, the December first opening I hoped for gets delayed because of slow delivery times due to the holidays. But while the women gear up for the event, I've been practicing my pizzas. Of course, my younger brothers are the test subjects.

To my surprise and astonishment, the dough is edible. They

compliment me on the toppings, and I don't find any of it in the trash.

Feeling good about the shop, despite the delay, I help bring Merry's pies to her stall at the Christmas bazaar.

"These look delicious," I say.

"Thank you. Your mom made that one. She's a quick learner. How are the pizzas going?"

"Gio said the one I made with the leftover meatballs that I cut into disks with red sauce, fresh mozzarella, shaved parmesan, cremini mushrooms, and oregano was his favorite."

She licks her lips. "I can't wait to try it. You should name it after your brother."

I set a pumpkin pie onto the folding table and then grip Merry's shoulders. "You are a genius. I'll name a pizza after each of my siblings." My mind flurries with inspiration. "I'll just have to get my mother's meatball recipe and the marinara sauce for authenticity. She does something toward the end of the long simmer that I've never been able to replicate."

"I have both," Merry says while adjusting the sign on her booth.

I almost fumble a pie. "You have both what?"

She arranges the pies on various stands across the tables. "Your mom gave me both recipes. I can give them to you."

I stand there frozen and very much blocking the way as she dodges around me, trying to get ready for the bazaar.

"Can you fasten this garland on the left? Does this look festive enough?" She surveys the table and then taps her finger on her chin as if it's missing something.

I'm certainly missing something. "Merry, my mother gave you her recipes?"

"Uh huh," she says like it's no big deal then spruces up the branches of a mini Christmas tree with fruit and pie-shaped decorations.

"She's never revealed her secrets to anyone, least of all her children. They're kept in a vault, under lock and key. We've lamented how she'll probably take whatever magic she works with those meatballs to the grave."

Merry taps my chest with her palm. "Well then, you're in luck. As I said, I have the recipes."

"Did you donate a kidney? Promise our firstborn? Make some kind of sacrifice?"

Her expression ripples with confusion then laughter. "Our what? No, I just taught her how to make a few basic pies. Let's see, she loved the caramel apple, the cherry, and the pumpkin praline." As if divesting the secret family recipe was no big deal, Merry stares at her display and then sighs. "Do you think we'll sell some pies today? I'm considering this a dry run for when we open shop and am worried people will be more interested in the custom Christmas tree decorations at the stall next to mine, the Bingo game, raffle, or the rummage sale."

"If these pies won my mother over, I'd be surprised if you have any remaining by noon. How many did you make?"

"Two dozen."

"Scratch that. You'll be sold out in an hour. May I recommend you get a clipboard and paper to take orders?"

"That's a great idea. Consider it a trade for the suggestion to name the pizzas after your siblings."

"Well, just be careful. Frankie came over last night and had a craving for baked beans and pickles. They do not belong on a pizza."

I tip my head back with laughter. Even though Merry wants to keep things in the *biz zone*, I can't help but fall more in love with this woman. She's smart, creative, and makes me laugh. Not to mention she's beautiful—her buttery, blonde hair is half up and cascades over her shoulders, her smooth skin, and her round, dimpled chin is purely kissable. I clear my throat so I don't say any of that out loud. "Duly noted."

The woman from the hallway at the resort when Merry and I ran into each other bustles over.

"Good morning, Mrs. Cringle," Merry says.

"Your table looks fantastic. Thank you for joining us on relatively short notice. I just knew everyone in Hawk Ridge Hollow had to have your pies. Tragic that your grandmother never opened a shop, but so excited that you are. Everyone is talking about it."

Merry and I both tuck our chins back.

"Really?" she asks.

"You know as well as anyone born and raised in this town that word spreads fast. I dare say like a snowball rolling downhill. A pizza-pie shop is sure to heat things up."

Nico pulls up and drops off my mother. She's not an angry woman by any stretch, but after having seven kids, she's often on her guard and isn't quick to smile. I won't deny my brothers and I were rascals. However, she lights up when she sees Merry, drawing her into a big hug.

To say I'm astounded is an understatement—not that I blame her. My affection for the Future Mrs. Costa is strong.

All I get from my mother is a simple, "Ciao, Tommy."

Merry makes introductions between the two older women. "Hello, Mrs. Costa. I'd like to introduce you to Mrs. Cringle. She makes the best cookies."

I can attest to this because when Mrs. Cringle saw us working at the shop the other day, she brought us some. They were the perfect balance of chew and crunch with oatmeal and butterscotch chips instead of chocolate.

"Merilee, I told you to call me Maria," my mom says then she and Mrs. Cringle start chatting.

"Seems like you won my mother over. I've never seen her so—"

Before I can pinpoint the right word to describe my mother's acceptance and affection for Merry, a woman with a deep tan plows into her.

I stiffen, ready to run interference when I recognize the person's voice.

"Oh, thank goodness you're here." Cassie wears sunglasses even though it's overcast. "Who knew Leon liked craft fairs." She rolls her eyes.

Slightly shaken and taken aback, Merry says, "Hi, Cassie. I didn't know you were back. Technically, this is a Christmas bazaar."

"Well, whatever, let's get out of here." Cassie tugs her hand. "I could use a spa treatment at the resort."

"I can't just leave. I have a stall here," Merry says.

Cassie chortles.

Merry gestures to the table.

"Seriously?"

"Seriously."

"Figures that our little House Mouse is still baking. If I had my way, I'd still be in Cancun, lounging on the beach and soaking up the sun. Hey, Tommy. You and Leon should hang out, considering you're also at a craft fair."

"Did you cut your honeymoon short?" I ask.

"No. Leon and I agreed that we'd do half and half. He didn't get to ski when we were here for the wedding, so we came back. Lucky for me, I married into wealth. Leon's dad has a private jet." She shimmies and waggles her eyebrows. "But if I had my way, we'd still be lounging poolside in the tropics."

"Marriage requires compromise sometimes. Ask my parents. They've been together for almost forty years. Mom loves to dance. Dad hates it. Naturally, they slow dance on their anniversary. Pop could go fishing all day every day. Live fish make Ma squirm, but she'll always be ready to cook his catch," I say.

"Aren't you wise, Tommy." Cassie's tone is bubbly sarcasm. "What are you doing here?"

I explain that Merry and I are opening a pizza and pie shop on Main Street.

She brushes her hands together. "Seriously?"

"Seriously," we repeat in unison.

Just then the jingling of copper bells followed by cheering grabs our attention. We turn around as four reindeer pulling a red sleigh approach, clearing a path through the stalls.

Santa Claus waves and tosses candy canes. Cassie catches one. Merry too.

"Santa winked at me. I think. Or he could've had something in his eye, but I'm pretty sure I got a wink," Merry says.

"Does that mean he saw your letter?" I ask, nudging her with my elbow.

"You wrote Santa a letter. Figures the little House Mouse would do something so quaint." Cassie clucks her tongue.

"Figuratively. Well, yes. It was more like a journal entry." Merry's grin transforms with confidence. "Cassie, you can call me House Mouse all day. I don't care. Seeing Santa makes me happy. People can argue that the guy in the red suit is fake or whatever. However, I choose to believe in the generosity of people. Kindness and goodness along with the possibility for miracles, especially at this time of year."

Cassie's expression filters through several emotions before it turns wistful, and she exhales through her nose. "Oh. Well..." She stammers as if not expecting Merry to hit the ball into the outfield by sticking up for herself.

"You're welcome to stick around, but I'd appreciate it if you speak to me more kindly," she adds.

"Is this about that handkerchief?"

"This is about how you've treated me since we were in college."

"How's that?" Cassie acts, flipping the sassy switch with her arms crossed in front of her chest.

"Like Merry is an irritating sibling who you're fine to hang out with until someone you think is cooler comes along then you try to make yourself look better by putting her down," I say in one breath.

"You're sticking up for her now?"

"Forever and always." I wrap my arm around Merry and draw her close then kiss the top of her head. It's a risk to be sure, but I want her to know we're a united front against the Cassies of the world.

Merry looks up at me with gratitude in her eyes. "Thanks."

"Anything for the Future Mrs. Costa."

"I always knew you two would be perfect for each other." She waggles her eyebrows then with a nervous laugh, indicating she's shifting from defensive to regretful, she adds, "I saw that marriage pact you guys made."

Merry's face falls. "Then why did you try to get with Tommy back in college?"

Cassie's right shoulder lifts slightly, and she stares at the snow-trodden ground. Clearing her throat, she says, "This isn't easy to admit, but I guess I was jealous. I saw the way he looked at you, waited for you, doted on you. How you were always so thoughtful and would get him a coffee on the way to class or leave jokes in his textbooks to make him laugh."

"And that made you want to keep us apart?" I ask, aghast.

"I was jealous is all." Cassie shrugs.

Merry leans in as if expecting her to explain or apologize.

"Yes, fine I'm sorry. I've felt bad all this time especially since we're frie-mily."

"Is that why you invited us both to your wedding?" Merry asks.

Her nod in response is slow, bashful.

Merry picks up one of the single slices of pie she's selling. "Thank you for saying you're sorry. Apology accepted. Here. Try this."

Cassie waves her away at the same time as my mother waves

goodbye to Mrs. Cringle and turns to us, her expression sharp in a way I recognize all too well—in much the same way I saw Cassie's angle. Having so many siblings has made me a quick study of human behavior. I'm guessing Ma heard the conversation. "You should have an entire pie, *signorina*. It'll sweeten the saltiness in you," she says, apparently having also overheard the accusation and apology from Cassie.

She takes it and has a bite because when my mother speaks, you listen. She chews for a long moment then her eyes light up. Around a mouthful, she says, "Wow. This is really good. No wonder Tommy fell in love with you."

Is it that obvious?

Merry's cheeks turn pink.

My gaze hovers on her until she looks up at me through her long lashes. A warm glow of certainty grows in my chest. Yes, Merry is the woman for me. It's meant to be. How could it not?

We all chat for a few more minutes, but when the Christmas bazaar crowd fills in, Merry and my mother take up their stations behind the table.

Fighting a desire to kiss Merry goodbye, I leave to head over to the shop to fire up the pizza oven—I inspected it and it's in great shape—work on some more recipes, wait for deliveries, and make sure Nico doesn't lag on his pizza box folding duties.

When I get to my truck, Rob Lasker from CoffeeHut leans against the driver's side door with his arms crossed.

"Can I help you?" My voice is more like a growl of warning than a polite inquiry.

"Listen, I'm sure you love your pizzas and that pie girl over there, but I'm going to make you an official offer to walk away."

My fists clench, ready to knock this guy over the tallest peak of the Hawk Ridge mountain range. "Walk away from Merry?"

He lets out a sharp breath. "I'll take her too. But I'm talking specifically about letting go of the commercial location on Main Street. I'll give you fifty grand to lock up and not look back."

"Not a chance."

"Seventy-five?"

Shaking my head slowly, menacingly, I tighten my left fist.

"One hundred thousand?" Rob asks.

I widen my stance, preparing to swing if this guy so much as says another word. Paulo would be proud.

Rob must read the anger coming off of me in hot waves because he feints to the right. "Okay, okay. Message received. You're not going to give up on your pathetic little pizza and pie shop."

"If I see you around here again, it won't just be these two fists that you'll find in your face."

The man lets loose a quavering laugh and then scurries away.

Still fuming when I get to the shop, I cool off by firing up the pizza oven and tinkering with the recipe I'll name after Merry, which includes caramelized onions, lightly grilled apples, bacon, goat cheese, thyme, and a light drizzle of maple syrup. My phone beeps with a text and rings at the same time, and I wipe my hands on the apron tied around my waist.

I answer when her name scrolls across the screen.

"Tommy, please come down to the bazaar. We have a problem." Alarm fills her voice.

Leaving Nico in charge with brief instructions not to burn the place down since the fire in the pizza oven is lit, I race over to the church parking lot. Cars line the street and the crowd has quadrupled since I left. There's hardly room to walk.

When I get to Merry's stall, this time, instead of her cheeks being pink from delightful embarrassment, they're flushed with distress.

"What happened?"

"Someone stole my pies," Merry says, holding her face in her hands. She explains that my mother was chatting with a potential customer while she was helping someone fill out the order form.

"When we were done, I turned around and the four pies I had left were gone."

My lips form a thin line. "Any idea who could've taken them?"

"I asked the people that were nearby, but with this crowd, they were busy too." She paces behind the empty table, fretting.

"On the upside, you nearly sold out in a few hours."

"And she has two dozen orders for the holidays," my mother adds. "But no one has any business stealing the pies."

Someone bumps into me and apologizes, reminding me of when Cassie crashed into Merry. "Do you think it could've been Cassie, making one last attempt to sabotage us?"

"I saw her and Leon leave. Plus, she ordered a pie. I guess they're spending Christmas at the resort and New Year's in Cancun."

I tuck my fist under my chin, thinking. "Hmm. Who else would've wanted to steal four pies?"

"Could've been two people," my mother says.

"I'm calling in the crew to help us investigate," I say, pulling out my phone.

"Do you mean your brothers?" Merry asks.

"What about your brothers?" a female voice asks from behind me.

"Oh, hi, Frankie," I say, sheepish.

"Whatever it is, I hope you were going to include your sister." She hoists Rafael higher on her hip.

Rusty brings up the rear with the other two kids who run to their grandmother.

I explain what happened with the stolen pies.

"People can be cutthroat." Frankie tells us a quick story about a rival restaurant when she still had hers in Manhattan.

"Could it be a rival bakery who got word about the shop?" Rusty asks.

"There's the Beanery, the Hawk & Whistle, and Mom &

Lollipop's, but I don't think they'd wish you ill will," Frankie says, peering around, ready to take down anyone who'd dare interfere with our enterprise. My sister may be the only girl and the youngest in the family, but she's easily as fierce as our mother.

"We'll go ask around," Rusty says. "Politely. Don't want this one taking off any heads." He places a gentle hand on his wife's shoulder.

"Oh, when I find out who took your pies, heads will roll," Frankie grinds out.

Merry starts to laugh then stops because Frankie's expression suggests that she's not joking.

Rusty wraps his arms around her and says, "Let's go find those warm, sweet, glazed mixed nuts you like so much before we do anything regrettable."

Frankie cranes her head back. With her two first fingers, she points to her eyes and then sweeps them at our surroundings, indicating that she'll be watching out for any perpetrators.

"You can take the woman out of New York City, but you can't take the city out of the woman," I say.

This time Merry does laugh.

"Don't worry. We'll figure it out," I say gently, wrapping my arm around her just like Rusty did to my sister.

She leans into me as if she needs a place to rest her worries. Then she abruptly pulls away. "Tommy, you're not trying to sabotage me, are you?"

I balk. "What? I'd never. Why would I do that? Why would you think that?" Something dense and heavy lands in my chest.

"So you can have the shop to yourself." Gazing down, she shuffles her foot on the ground.

"You heard Marley's ultimatum," I retort, defensive.

"Sorry, I just worried that you—"

"Have I given you a reason not to trust me?"

"I saw you talking to Coffee Breath earlier."

"Yeah, I was telling him that there's no—" I go quiet as realization dawns. "Rob Lasker, that creep. He's the pie thief." I tell Merry about our conversation, leaving out how close I was to knocking out the jerk with a simple jab and cross.

"Maybe we should include him in 'The Twelve Dishes of Christmas.' One slice seemed to work with Cassie," Merry suggests.

I glower. "The only thing that guy will be getting is a pie to the face."

"We don't need an assault charge on top of everything."

My shoulders remain tense, but I soften slightly. "Leave that to Frankie. But don't worry. We'll kill him with kindness before any swings are taken."

"By kill him with kindness do you mean drive Coffee Breath and his CoffeeHut van out of Hawk Ridge Hollow?"

"Exactly."

I don't see Merry for the rest of the day as I patrol the town, searching for the black van. By evening, half the residents have their eyes out for Rob Lasker. I hear numerous stories about how poorly CoffeeHut treats its workers, that they don't contribute to the towns and cities where they have their stores, and that there's a rumor of tax fraud.

When I go to sleep that night, I calm myself by thinking of the different pizzas I'll make to name after my siblings in addition to Frankie's menu. It weaves into my dreams where I'm tossing dough, cooking them in the woodfired pizza oven, and serving them to happy customers.

Then I wake to the sound of sirens.

CHAPTER 13

MERILEE

In the middle of the night, I wake up to pounding on the door and a man hollering my name. Dazed and groggy, I make my way out of bed. As I pass through the kitchen, the oven clock says that it's four am. The silhouette of a large and familiar figure in a green parka with a faux fur-lined hood stands on the front porch.

"Tommy, what's wrong?" I ask as I pull open the door.

He steps back, relief streaking across his otherwise pained expression. "You're okay. You're here."

"What's the matter?"

He scrubs his hand down his face. "There was a fire in town."

"Is everyone okay?"

His eyes bore into me. "Yes. Thank goodness you're okay."

My stomach clenches with worry. "Was it at the shop?"

"Someone set fire to the wooden loading area in the back. It started to spread to the exterior of the kitchen, but the fire department got there in time. They cleared the building, but—"

My hand presses to my mouth. "But—?" I ask, terrified of what he's going to say next.

"But I worried you were there early, baking. That I could've lost you." His breath puffs in the cold air.

"After the long day at the bazaar, I couldn't quite bring myself to begin my baker's hours."

Tommy's stature is tense, his eyes wide and sharp.

"Do you want to come inside and warm up?"

"No." His tone is gruff.

Slightly taken aback, I say, "Okay. Glad everything is under control."

"Sorry. That was...intense. We'll have to take deliveries through the front until we replace the rear entrance. Thankfully, it won't affect the rest of the shop."

"Is there anything I can do to help?" I ask.

Tommy shakes his head. "We have another full day ahead. I'll see you in a few hours."

"Thanks for checking on me and for letting me know what happened."

Without another word, Tommy returns to his truck, idling in my driveway.

I climb back into bed but can't sleep. My mind races with questions about how the fire started and speculation about what could've happened.

Repeatedly, my thoughts return to the man standing on my front porch. I've never seen Tommy so distraught, so upset—not even after he told me about Rob Lasker's offer. This was different. Tension and rage burned inside of him. I worry he's mad at me, but that's silly. I didn't do anything wrong.

It's then I realize that had the building burned down, it would've taken his business with it. Who knows how the fire started, but if I made a mistake and left an oven on or something else went wrong, I'd be to blame, sending Tommy and his dream to have the family working at the pizza shop up in flames.

This is why I made up the rule that we can't date. As much as I want to be the Future Mrs. Costa, the shop brings too much responsibility. There are too many ways it could fail, driving a wedge between our friendship.

I have to protect it and my heart even though he fills mine to overflowing with the way he looks at me a second longer than anyone else then flashes a half-smile like he knows something I don't. How, so far, he crosses every *T* and dots every *I* to make sure the restaurant bakery will be legit. And how he calls me Merry. Only Nan and Grampa ever used that nickname. It makes me feel special.

But *we* cannot be. We can't risk hurting each other because of how it could ruin our goals, crush our dreams.

When I get to the shop a few hours later, I find Tommy in the kitchen, talking quietly with the fire chief.

"Hi, Chief Hawkins," I say. "Thank you for everything."

"You guys are lucky we got here when we did."

I'm afraid to see the damage, but the interior of the kitchen looks perfectly intact even though soot coats the rear windows.

"And thank you for the info, Tommy. Makes me happy to know there are good men like you with experience and know-how even if you're no longer in a company. Your station was lucky to have you."

"Just doing my duty, sir."

And so am I. Keeping things professional is my responsibility as a business owner. As attracted to Tommy as I am, I have to resist him. A stilted breath escapes as what I want and what I know is right slices me into pieces.

As Tommy walks Chief Hawkins to the door, the two confer in low voices.

I wonder if Tommy knows more about what happened than he's letting on.

After Chief Hawkins leaves, Tommy lingers in the front for a long moment and his broad shoulders lift and lower on a sigh.

"Any idea what caused the fire?" I ask.

He takes a long moment to answer. "Very likely an arsonist."

I gasp. "In Hawk Ridge Hollow?"

He gives me a dry and technical explanation of the signs that indicate someone set the fire and it wasn't due to the pizza oven coals, a problem with the electricity, or any number of other ways it could've started.

"Why would someone start a fire back there? Who?"

"The pie thief?" he asks rhetorically.

"Coffee Breath?"

"Yes, Chief Hawkins is investigating Rob Lasker."

My pulse shortens. "But one of us could've been inside. Someone could've been hurt."

"Merry, we need to talk."

My vision turns cloudy as I fear everything falling apart before we've even gotten started, given it a chance.

"You were right," Tommy says.

I tuck my head back, not sure what he means.

"Despite the pact, my parents wanting us to get married, and what Marley said, you were right. We can't run this place and be together. There's too much at risk. I don't want to lose our friendship or the shop...or you."

I nod as time slows. Deep down I don't want Tommy to give up on us even though I'm the one who initially said we shouldn't be together. But it's the responsible thing. I tell myself I'm glad he realized that.

His nostrils flare and his lips press together like he's ready to fight, only this time, with himself. "I'm sorry. What happened this morning was—"

"I understand. We have to focus on the business."

Tommy gazes toward the dirty windows in the back. "If

that's what you think is best," he says as if second-guessing or distracted by the close call with the fire.

"Of course. As you said, I was right."

He grunts.

"I'd better get to work. We have the grand opening coming up and the 'Twelve Dishes of Christmas' too."

"I'm expecting a few deliveries today as well."

We both nod slowly, almost in sync. Then I wave. It's just a little wave like maybe the kind I'd give to a baby if it were looking at me. But yeah, I wave, reminding me of my bow not too long ago.

Not at all awkward. Definitely not a cringe-worthy moment. Except it is painfully so because, again, this feels like a goodbye.

Now I shake my head because I have to somehow stop myself from making this worse. Tommy mimics me slowly, confusedly.

I wag my finger side to side. "Nnnnn." The beginning of the word no comes out of my mouth but gets stuck before the vowel.

"Nnnnn?" he asks.

I run into the kitchen, contemplating stuffing my head in a snowbank outside. There are plenty now. I wanted to say, No, no I don't like the new plan, but I forced myself to hold back. It's for the best. Right?

As I organize the baking area of the kitchen, I mix up the labels for the different flours, dump out a bag of icing sugar, and nearly stab myself with a pair of scissors while unpacking one of the deliveries.

I find the banner we ordered for the front of the building that says Hawk Ridge Hollow Pizza & Pie that'll be temporary until we have the wooden one made. I wish we could come up with a slightly more original name for this place. Funny, how that was always the hang-up that kept me from pursuing this dream. Yet here I am.

Tommy and I work in silence, only speaking to each other when necessary. Our chatter, banter, and easy rapport are absent.

Like in college, after I walked in on him and Cassie, it's like we're drifting apart. Only this time, it seems more like his doing.

Can I forgive myself if I lose Tommy again? Will I be able to move on?

My thoughts hum with a single syllable that starts with the letter *N* and ends with the letter *O*. The simple word that I tried to say before but couldn't.

But I have no choice. I have to let him go.

For better or worse, I don't sleep much for the next few days. Instead, I bake, practicing recipes. I wish I could say that I sampled as I went, but I've lost my appetite. Even though we weren't together, it's like Tommy and I broke up. Only, it was a mutual decision, initiated by me. Confirmed by him.

Well, Santa, I guess I got what I wanted...and gave it up.

I should feel better about remaining friends only. Instead, my heart sags, beats slowly, and longs for something more. Longs for Tommy.

Like the bottom of a soggy pie, I droop through the days, preparing for the grand opening of the shop. I botch two orders —swapping key lime for lemon meringue. I forget to include pie tins when Tommy places another order with the restaurant supply company. It's just the container that literally holds a pie together. No biggie.

I scour the local thrift stores, church basements, friends' attics, and the market to collect as many pie plates as I can until we get the aluminum kind delivered.

Meanwhile, I feel like I'm falling apart. Parts of me flaking off. Other parts are claggy and cakey. It's like I'm clogged up and spilling all over the place, completely out of sorts.

Can someone be lovesick? If so, I've got it everywhere, inside and out. Every pore, hair, and fiber of my being afflicts me, especially my heart. I should climb into bed and not leave. Where's my fluffy robe when I need it?

When I pull up to the shop that evening because I forgot Nan's recipe box, the soft overhead lights glow as Tommy and his brothers bustle around inside, preparing for the soft opening tomorrow with family and friends.

My heart tugs because I've always wanted a family—loud, boisterous, loving. I could be the Future Mrs. Costa. I adore Tommy's parents. His mother is what I imagined mine was like. She and Nan would've been best friends. At first glance, his dad seems like a gruff, no-nonsense mafia boss, but is as friendly as any Hawk Ridge Hollow local. Frankie and her brothers are each unique, and I'd be honored to call them siblings-in-law.

But I can't let what I want interfere with what I need—keeping Tommy's friendship and the pie shop.

It was fun while it lasted.

Now, it's back to business.

Instead of going through the front, I sneak through the back even though it's still under repair. Strangely, the rear window is open and what looks like one of my pies sits on the windowsill.

When I enter, Nico scoots past. "Hey, Merilee." He disappears into the walk-in fridge.

A camera sits on the prep table and the red light blinks. I gaze into it. "Is this thing on?"

Considering all the activity I saw through the front windows only moments ago, the shop is now unusually quiet.

When Nico doesn't come out of the fridge for a concerning amount of time and voices echo from inside, I poke my head in the door.

Four Costa brothers sit atop overturned milk crates, gazing intently at a computer screen.

"I should've been a spy," Nico says.

"If it works," Tommy says.

"Hey, Merilee," Nico repeats as if whatever is happening is completely normal.

"Are you filming a commercial or something for the shop?"

"No, we're trying to catch a thief," Gio says.

"And an arsonist," Tommy mutters.

"Wait, my brother didn't tell you—?" Luca starts.

Tommy elbows him hard.

"What? I figured she'd know what you're up to."

Without tearing his gaze from the computer screen, Tommy says, "Last night we set a trap."

"We put a weighted alarm on the windowsill with what looks like a pie on top," Nico says proudly.

"Did someone try to take it?"

"A raccoon," Luca says. "But it didn't set off the alarm."

"I'm working on it," Nico says, adjusting something on the computer program.

"Merilee should go over to the window, set the pie down," he pauses and does air quotes, "and loudly say, 'I have to leave this pie to cool. Do you think it's safe to leave the window open overnight?'"

"Great plan," Luca says with a roll of his eyes.

"Do you have something better, genius?" Tommy asks.

Face no doubt wrinkled with confusion, I say, "And why should I do all that?"

"Because the culprit will think we've left the place unattended, get up to no good, and we'll catch them red-handed," Tommy says.

I tap the air with my finger. "Makes perfect sense since the citizens of Hawk Ridge Hollow are criminals who regularly steal pies. *Not*. Listen, I know I mentioned that Old Man Orson was about as friendly as a wart, but he wouldn't—"

Tommy's elbows rest on his knees and he clutches his fist

with his hand. "The culprit isn't a citizen of this town. I'm certain it's Rob Lasker."

"Coffee Breath from Coffee Hut?" I ask.

"Their coffee is sludge," Gio says.

"Why wouldn't they go after the Beanery?" Nico asks.

"Because they want to rent this place. Marley probably told him that he gave us an ultimatum and now Rob is trying to run us out of town."

I clap my hands together, not quite sure what to make of this scene and lamenting that even though Tommy and I ditched the possibility of having a relationship, we haven't quite returned to our regular friendship status. "Okay boys, I'm going to leave you to your stakeout."

Gio clicks his tongue and to Tommy, he says, "Frankie is going to be ticked that you're skipping out on card night."

"We can have it here," he answers.

"All of us in the walk-in?" Nico asks.

"Why was she invited to play again?" Tommy asks.

"Because she's our sister. Once you and Merry get married, are you really telling me you'll exclude her from card night?" Nico says.

Tommy and I both start talking at once.

He lets me speak. "Oh, we're not getting married. Figured it would be too difficult, what with running this place and catching thieves." The words are like reciting lines—a story I've told myself and not at all true. They're much like shouting, 'I have to leave this pie to cool. Do you think it's safe to leave the window open overnight?'

"It's what makes the most sense," Tommy says flatly.

I bunch my hands in front of my chest so they don't see that my heart is about to burst through to announce the truth that I want to be with Tommy. Then again, I've never known him to be so cold, so distant, and harsh.

"So that's why you've been acting like a caveman," Luca says.

Gio's cheeks puff up and he lets out a long breath.

Nico shakes his head slowly as if warning against proceeding with this conversation.

I thumb over my shoulder. "Well, I should probably go set the fake pie on the windowsill." I leave the walk-in fridge and select a chocolate cream pie because maybe the criminal needs some sweetness in their life like Mrs. Costa said about Cassie. Either that or it'll topple onto their head, catching them cream-faced. Speaking in a loud, clear voice, I speak the lines about leaving the pie and then go to my car.

When I get home, I recall that I went to the shop to get my grandmother's recipe box that I'd left behind earlier. Unfortunately, preoccupied with Tommy and the stakeout, I forgot to grab it.

There was one pie I've never tried making—the 'Razzle dazzle merry berry buttermilk pie.' It was my Grampa's favorite. Nan made it on birthdays, anniversaries, and holidays only. Although, I do recall she'd sometimes make it just because, especially when Grampa got sick.

Once, I asked him why he liked it so much and he said it was the pie of his heart, specially made by the woman of his heart. I warm at the thought and the love they shared.

I wonder if there's a pie of Tommy's heart. I trace back through these last weeks and college, recalling what he likes to eat besides pizza. Then I remember the big smile on his face when he talked about tiramisu.

The next day, I oversleep and get to the shop late. The guys are already there, arranging tablecloths, stocking the drink machine, and the pizza oven blazes.

Everyone is so busy, that I don't get a chance to ask about the results of the "pie-out" and if they caught the culprit. I wouldn't be at all surprised if they grilled steak so they could say it was a stakeout.

The corners of Tommy's lips lift into a smile, but he doesn't direct it at me. In fact, he makes every effort not to look at me. When I ask him if the pie tins were in the latest delivery, I glance over my shoulder because he fixates on something behind me.

Is this what rejection is like? I feel about as small as a house mouse and wouldn't mind finding a hole to sneak into.

"We got some footage last night," he says. "A guy dressed in black...and a black van leaving the rear lot."

"That's good, right? Did you send it to the authorities?"

"Sure did and Chief Hawkins called and said he has some info for us."

The word *us* cuts into me. Then Nan's voice interrupts my desire to scamper away. She taught me that I have to give what I want to get. In this case, a simple, friendly conversation with Tommy.

Nevertheless, I clasp my hands and nervously twist them in front of me. "You never told me what made you want to be a firefighter."

The sadness in his eyes conflicts with the faint smile on his lips. "To be of service, educate and help people, and to save lives."

"That's very honorable. What made you leave?"

Tommy's expression scatters in a direction that I cannot follow.

The pizza pan in his hands clatters to the counter. "Sorry. Butterfingers. I, uh, I don't talk about that."

My chest tightens because I can see he's upset and as his friend, as someone who cares for and loves this man, I want to ease whatever pains him.

My heart surges in my chest. Yes, I love him. So much it almost hurts.

"Sure. I understand." I turn to go back to the baking section of the kitchen then stop short. "Well, if you ever do want to talk about it, I'm here. That's what friends are for."

All the Costas except Paulo join us for the soft opening along with a few of my friends, Clive and Margie from Hawk Ridge Hollow Helpers, Mrs. Cringle, her sisters, Tobias Marley, and many members of the Hawkins family. Gloria, who's a ray of sunshine to Bruno's typical gloomy, grumpy numbers guy, brings each of the Costa family members a handknit mini stocking stuffed with candy. I get one too. Joy who has been helping Gio in the front sits next to him, and I wonder just how cozy they've been getting.

Tommy's brothers and Frankie applaud and tease him in equal measure about the pizzas named after them. There's even "The Merry"—a savory variation on my favorite sweet pie, containing apples and bacon. This makes me think of the pie I've been working on during the nights when I can't sleep, but I probably won't call it "The Tommy." It's more like the pie of my heart.

Overall, the opening is a smashing success with lots of food and drink, a functional dishwasher, and compliments on our logo that's half pizza half pie. Everything is perfect except for one thing.

Tommy never speaks directly to me. He gives a speech, thanking everyone for helping out, spreading the word, and bringing the shop to life. While we dish out slices of pizza and pie alike, give toasts, and chat with our guests, we never cross paths. Every time I try to get his attention, he's called in a different direction.

Frankie sits in the window with her feet up on an empty chair and her hand on her belly.

"Ready to burst?" Nico asks as he busses the table.

She playfully whacks her brother as he scoots away.

"No, I ate too much pie. I think I had a slice of each. Merilee, you're an amazing baker. I'm excited that you're going to be my sister-in-law."

I shift uncomfortably.

"And not only because of the pie. Though the dessert game at family gatherings just significantly improved. Ma and Pop aren't bakers."

"Tommy didn't tell you?" I wring my hands.

She meets my eyes. "Gio did. We played cards last night and Tommy lost. Never happens. I knew something was up. Made him spill the beans." She taps her chin. "I could go for some baked beans and pickles right now."

"I thought you were full from the pie?"

"These cravings don't make sense. Anyway, next time you talk to my brother—" Frankie speaks with Costa confidence. As if Tommy and I are still friends and she has no doubt I'm still the Future Mrs. Costa. Wish I had that kind of confidence.

"Which one?"

"Tommy." She lifts her eyebrows as if that's obvious. "Have him tell you why he's no longer climbing ladders and putting out fires."

"He said he doesn't talk about it."

"But you're his best friend and future wife, of course, he'll tell you."

"I'm not so sure about that." I tell Frankie about the so-called human resource policy and my recent conversation with Tommy.

She rolls her eyes. "He's scared of losing you. You're scared of well, you tell me, but speaking from experience, you can figure out a solution. Look who I married—he won the award for least likely to interact with another human being several years running."

"Rusty was a full-on mountain man?"

"All grizzly. Like Rusty, my brothers aren't always forthcoming with their emotions. Some of them don't want to marry and settle down because they're being stupid and stubborn—an undesirable family trait. You've been warned. Others haven't found the right person. But Tommy met the right person at the wrong time. Now, I daresay that it's the right person and right time. That person is you."

Something settles inside at her words, at hearing the truth. The one I've been fighting because she's right. I am scared. "But how do I tell him that?"

"You show him, I guess. Do what you do best."

"Bake him a pie?" I ask because as it turns out, I have a sweet little work in progress.

"I meant just be yourself."

I shift uncomfortably because I'm over thirty and only now starting to accept who I am, quirky, cringy, introvert, and all.

Frankie doesn't tell me anything else about the inner workings of her brother's mind. However, back home later that night, while I continue to work on the tiramisu pie, I realize maybe there is a solution.

I could approach our romance, our love story, like a pie recipe. If the ratio of flour and butter is off, it can be too cakey, tough, or not flakey enough. Warm pie dough can cause the crust to break. Forget salt and the outcome is bland. Not enough sugar, the dough doesn't quite crisp properly. Then when it comes to the fillings, they can wobble, spillover, burst through, or fall flat. Whether I add sugar, spice, or salt to the recipe, it all has to be in balance. Same with things between Tommy and me.

I've recovered from numerous pie fails, and this is no different, right?

As I sprinkle a light dusting of cocoa in the shape of a heart over the creamy tiramisu filling, I wonder if the pie recipe I concocted out of the traditional dessert could be the key to Tommy's heart. I have to give to get. Show him my love, that I want a future for us, and prove to myself that I'm willing to push past my fears, out of my comfort zone, and do it scared.

If I can travel the world on various missions, compete in a baking contest, and open a pie shop with little experience, surely, I can do this.

I'm done running away from love. Subtly sabotaging myself so I don't have to commit to things. Being afraid that the people I care about will be taken away from me.

The alternative, a lonely and loveless life, is worse than my fears.

It's time for me to roll up my sleeves, put on my big girl pants, and House Mouse the heck out of Tommy Costa.

The next day, I call Tommy and ask him to meet me at the Beanery.

I spot him through the window, head down against the wind, hands in pockets, expression crushed. He straightens and pulls off his hat when he enters the café, tousling his dark hair. Stubble lines his jaw and his dark eyes dart around sharply before landing on me.

My lips tremble and butterflies body slam each other in my belly. This could go wonderfully or be the end.

I repeat Nan's words. *Give to get. Give to get.* I want to be courageous and overcome my fears of rejection and abandonment. I want Tommy to do the same so we can be together.

"Why'd we meet here and not at the shop?" His voice is rough.

I hold out his usual coffee order in a paper cup. "Because I wanted to meet as friends, not as business partners."

He half-sits on the stool at one of the high-top tables as if ready to flee.

"Get comfortable. This might take a minute."

"What's up?" he asks.

"I was wrong."

"I distinctly remember telling you that you were right."

"Ordinarily, I'd like hearing those two magical words, but in this instance, I mistakenly believed that I couldn't have the business and a relationship with you because we'd lose our friendship." I gaze at my hands, willing the resolve to speak honestly, the way friends do, the way I'd like him to speak to me. "And afraid that if I let someone get too close, I'll lose them. Like I did with Nan and Grampa along with my parents. Those losses were so hard to bear that a scared part of my brain told me I could have one or the other and if I chose you, I'd lose you as well."

Tommy takes a slow sip of his coffee. "That makes zero sense but perfect sense too. I, uh, understand."

"Do you though? Because last time I checked, you have a very large and very alive family."

Tommy remains quiet for a beat and his espresso brown eyes flicker with sadness. "A little over a year ago, I was on a call. Bad fire. I lost—" His voice chokes off. "I couldn't get them out. Tried. Tried until I could no longer breathe. Until I was spent. Until I almost died."

My hand flies to his and grips it tight. "I'm sorry. So sorry."

"As a result, I sustained significant lung damage. Had to take a desk job or retire. Missed my family. Moved here." The words are choppy, hard for him to speak.

My throat tightens, feeling for him.

"My whole identity was wrapped up in being a firefighter. If I can't save people, who am I? What could I do? The night of the fire on the loading dock, I spooked. Afraid if something happened, I wouldn't be strong enough to save you. What if something happened to you?" His eyes flick to mine, hollow with terror.

"Can I talk to you, friend to friend?" I ask.

"I thought that's what we're doing."

"You are the biggest, strongest, toughest guy I know. There's a reason your brothers listen to you, and it's not only because they respect you. If you wanted, you could knock 'em back to New York City."

Tommy chuckles. "I have injuries, Merry. My lungs aren't what they used to be."

"And we're not what we used to be."

"I know. These few days have been weird. I don't like not talking with you, laughing with you...kissing you."

A smile teases my lips. "I really like those things too. All this time, I've been thinking like Merry from college—who could've talked to you about everything that happened with Cassie and saved myself a lot of heartache."

"Heartache?"

"Years' worth. I had a crush on you, but it wasn't until you were no longer part of my daily life that realized that I should've told you."

His eyes twinkle. "Same. So do you mean to say that we're not the same people we used to be, but we've been acting like we are?"

"Yeah. Like having this conversation, right now. Pretty mature, right? As I said, we're not the same people as we were in college, but I believe we can be even better. Don't you think?"

"We were pretty awesome."

I slide off my stool and closer to him, leaning against his knees. "But I want something more, Tommy. I want to stick to the pact."

"The business pact or the marriage pact? Because I've been really hoping that you'd come around and realize you can have your pie and eat it too."

I giggle. "Good one. And yes, the Future Mrs. Costa pact. But I have an amendment to make. We have to promise to communicate no matter how hard it is."

"I think that's covered in the no secrets clause."

"Fair enough. So do you think we can let ourselves love even if it means the possibility of someday losing each other? Because the time between now and then seems like it would really stink—worse than the you-know-what in the shop's bathroom—without you in it."

The corner of Tommy's lips twist with a smile. "Yes. A hundred times yes. These last few days have been miserable."

"Same. We got this. Now, let's blow this popcorn stand, er, coffee shop."

He tilts his head with laughter at our old catchphrase. Then we finish our drinks and wander, hand in hand, toward our pizza and pie place.

Clusters of Christmas trees line the street, wreaths with red bows hang on all the wrought iron lantern posts, and garlands of glowing snowflakes crisscross overhead. The fresh dusting of snow makes the colorful lights on the bushes look like giant gumdrops.

Officer Owen Hawkins talks to his brother, Chief Hawkins, in front of the shop.

"We were just looking for you. Good news, your pie saved the day," the fire chief says.

"We were able to connect the pie thief from the church Christmas bazaar to the arsonist to the windowsill pie thief using cellphone geolocation data," Owen adds.

"Don't tell me it was Old Man Orson because I've been wanting to go sledding and intended to bribe him with a pie." My lips twist as if to say aw-shucks.

Owen chuckles. "No, it was Robert J. Lasker. He was a CoffeeHut employee and had a bit of record as an extortionist. Now, we can bring him up on a few more charges."

"Thank you for your hard work," Tommy says.

"So no more attempts at Coffee Breath trying to sabotage us?" I ask.

"She means Rob Lasker," Tommy clarifies.

"No. He's been arrested. In fact, there's a bill in the works to restrict the use of commercial space on Main Street to privately owned businesses only so no big corporations will darken our doorsteps."

"I take it Mr. Marley paid his taxes."

"And then some. The bill is titled 'The Judy Marley Provision.'"

We talk to them for a few more minutes and then go inside the shop.

"What a relief that's over," I say, straightening a tablecloth.

"Ciao, CoffeeHut."

"Coffee Breath," I mutter.

Tommy chuckles. "Are you ready for tomorrow?"

"The grand opening? I have a bit of baking to do. I've been working on a special pie. It's called Tommy's Tiramisu." I take a few steps closer to him. Then I tell him about Grampa's "Razzle dazzle merry berry buttermilk pie."

"Sounds delicious. I hear the Hawk Ridge Hollow Sweetheart is quite the pie baker."

"Oh, you're digging up that old title?"

He wraps his hands around my waist, sending a thrill through me. "If it fits...and it does perfectly. But I want to know, why'd you ditch it? You're quite the sweetheart if you ask me."

"I guess I never thought of myself that way. I put myself in a box—Nan's granddaughter, an orphan, quiet, alone...lonely. It was easier to be small than to face all my big emotions." And I so badly want to let them go and accept who I am—quiet when I'm thinking about Nan and baking or loud and loving when I'm with the Costas. It can be both.

Tommy brushes his thumb across my chin. "You do see how beautiful you are, right?"

I lift a shoulder in a shrug.

"Well, I do, so you'd better get used to me ogling you, whispering sweet nothings in your ear, sneaking a kiss...and you know what they say about Italian guys? They like to pinch." He makes a pinching motion with his fingers and goes for what Frankie calls the tooshie.

I giggle and yelp as he chases me around the restaurant. Then he captures me in his arms and tips me back slightly. Our gazes meet and hold. Oh, those espresso eyes warm me up and melt me down. I suppose I can let myself be loved by Tommy. Actually, there's no choice but to see myself the way he sees me if this relationship is going to work.

I sink into his arms and smile, free at last.

"Any chance I can taste test that pie you mentioned?" he asks.

"Sure can. And by the way, I had a slice of the 'The Merry' pizza yesterday and it was my favorite."

"I was hoping you'd like it. So, we're going to do this?"

"Do you mean this?" I straighten and gesture to the shop. "Or this?" I wag my finger between us.

"Both."

"Yes, I'm berry, berry ready."

He gives me a flirty half-smile. "Did you say berry?"

"Sure did. I love you to pizzas, Tommy."

Now, he flashes a full smile. "Pieces?"

"Sure do."

"Merry, have I ever told you that pie love you berry much?"

This time I giggle. "I think our grandkids are going to love your jokes."

"How about we start with kids?"

"Marriage first?"

"Definitely."

Tommy loops his pinky around mine, drawing me closer. He plants one palm on my jaw and the other on my waist. I meet his espresso brown eyes long enough to know this is real and there's no going back. Not to college. Not to last week. There's only forward, together.

His lips land softly on mine in a kiss that's stronger than a pact. It's a promise to always be honest, true, not to keep secrets or share a toothbrush, and to always put the toilet seat down, and maybe I'll leave it up for him from time to time.

I can live with that compromise as long as it's a life with Tommy.

EPILOGUE

*D*ear Santa,

It's me again. I have a few updates since I last checked in. The pizza and pie shop is up and running—we've been slammed with customers, which is a good thing. It's long hours, but I already feel like we're family.

Additionally, in the twelve days leading up to Christmas, we made 'The Twelve Dishes of Christmas' secret Santa deliveries of pizzas and pies to twelve local families and establishments. Hope you don't mind that we borrowed your name. We brought one to Mr. Marley who recently reunited with his daughter and grandkids. I'm guessing they've been very good this year. Just saying. Oh, and Frankie and Rusty's four children are rascally little angels. Yes, Frankie had her baby. Another girl and they named her Carlina. She's adorable and so squishable.

Where was I? Oh, yes. We also donated to the workers at the animal shelter, Hawk Ridge Hollow Helpers, the nurses and staff at the medical center, the church along with the firemen and police officers at the new safety complex. I'm forgetting a few, but you get the gist. I hope I'm still on the good list.

I may be too old to write you, but I'm not too old to go sledding down Old Man Orson's hill. I brought him Nan's famous Tollhouse Cookie Pie, so he didn't chase us out of the snow. Speaking of *us*...

Thank you for the early Christmas gift. Wouldn't you know, I woke up on Christmas morning to find a very large present curled up under my tree. He even had a bow on top of his head. It was a miracle, I tell ya!

Actually, Tommy (yes, the one from college) made me pretend it was Christmas morning on Christmas Eve, pajamas and all. He made a sorry excuse for a rooster's crow so I'd "wake" up. Nadine and her kids who are staying with me for the holidays were not amused.

I wandered out to find the tree glowing and beneath it, the guy of my dreams. You did an exceptional job with this gift. He's cute, my age, has thick hair, and a great smile.

Oh, he's also really skilled at eating pie...and as it turns out, making pizza. So it's a win-win. We're always equipped with dinner and dessert.

So, the problem is solved. I'm no longer lonely. In fact, I have a big family now. Actual Christmas Day was sheer (and delicious) chaos. But I got another unexpected gift.

After supper (indulge me for a moment because I need to relive the meal), consisting of a charcuterie board—that was the king, er, I should say the queen of charcuterie boards since Mrs. Costa made it—that even included fresh truffles. Plus, manicotti with pesto Genovese, homemade lobster ravioli, carbonara, shrimp scampi, slow-cooked meats, and don't even get me started on the bread.

As I was saying, after we had our fill, Tommy dragged everyone out of the house for a walk that led us to the pizza and pie shop. I instantly noticed the vinyl sign was gone, replaced with one that says *Costa's Pizza and Pie*.

I winced and looked up at Tommy, worried, and said, "Shouldn't it say *Costa & Ketchum Pizza and Pie?*"

Then he dropped to one knee and said, "I'm hoping you'll become Mrs. Costa." Then he presented a sparkling Duchess set engagement ring and asked me to marry him.

Of course, I said yes. We hugged (and kissed) then he said, "*I want this to be a Marry Christmas, Merry.*"

Given the audience, everyone laughed and offered their congratulations. So, next time you hear from me, I'll no longer be the Future Mrs. Costa, but Merilee Costa. Just in case, you know, you need that information for deliveries.

Love,
Merilee (aka Complete with a Santa of my own)

P.S. Here's a pie for you and the missus. I have a feeling she'll enjoy it.

P.P.S. In case you're wondering, Mr. and Mrs. Costa received a check in the mail from the Liegerian prince, "paying them back" with a note that looked strangely like Tommy's handwriting and said *Please don't loan me money again.* Strange, right?

P.P.P.S. I'm sure glad I still have Nan's handkerchief with the blue embroidered *C*. I guess it was meant to be mine.

SNEAK PEEK AT GLORIA & BRUNO AND THE FIVE GOLDEN RINGS

Chapter 1 Gloria

I've never met a cookie I didn't like, and I hope I can say the same is true for my new landlord. I thank Mrs. Cringle from the Welcome Center for the assortment I'm bringing as a reverse housewarming gift. A bell jingles as I exit the little popup Christmas cookie shop on my way into Hawk Ridge Hollow.

Despite the last few months, the skip returns to my step. Must be the holly jolly area or that it's so cold. But that I can live with.

What kind of town constructs a small cabin at its foothills to welcome seasonal visitors to enjoy a sweet treat, cocoa, get pictures with Santa, and view a display of the local offerings?

The perfect town, that's what. The one I bravely decided to up and move to, sight unseen. The same goes for my apartment, but if it's anything like Hawk Ridge Hollow, I'll be fine.

No, I'll be over the moon.

This place is straight out of a Hallmark movie. The snow-lined streets, the Christmas lights are strewn and sparkling on the trees, the window displays in the shops, and the mixed scents of cinnamon, chocolate, and cider swirling in the air.

I'm home.

Well, not quite, but I'm on my way as I continue down Main Street. Then, according to the directions, I'll have to make a few turns to arrive at Acorn Lane. It's not exactly walkable, but that's okay.

This place is so cute! So quaint! I cannot wait to see my new apartment.

But first, I slowly cruise past a candy shop, a jewelry store with a snowflake and shimmer theme, Mrs. Cringle's Toys & Crafts—the woman at the welcome center must own it. There's the Hawk & Whistle Pub, a general store, and library—trimmed for Christmas with a giant wreath made of books. In the distance, ribbons of ski trails lead to the Hawk Ridge Hollow Resort nestled at the base of the mountain.

Now I understand why this was my father's favorite place to visit when he was a kid. Too bad we weren't able to come here as a family. I'll have to call my brother Dominic after I get settled and tell him all about it. I cannot wait for him to visit closer to Christmas.

There will be plenty of time to explore after I unpack and start work on Monday. I'm so excited that I'm practically vibrating.

At the top of my voice, I sing along to the Christmas song on the radio and almost miss the GPS's instructions to turn onto Acorn Lane.

In fact, it's so narrow, I'm lucky I don't drive past it. It should be called Acorn Alley, wedged between two brick buildings that are more industrial with the crumbling old brick and sparse windows and less residential than I'd like. But who knows, it may open up to a clearing surrounded by oak trees, park benches, and squirrels scurrying around. Am I in fantasyland? Yes, indeed, and I don't mind a bit. On second thought.

perhaps this is a shortcut, and the street is more easily accessed at the other end if there's easier access.

I should probably find out, considering I'm driving a massive pickup truck. Figured Cole wouldn't miss it too much. Once upon a time, he played the role of urban cowboy, wearing boots and driving this truck. Before that, he was into athletic gear, drank protein shakes all day, and constantly flexed in the mirror when he didn't think anyone was looking. I should've spotted the pattern. Now, he probably drives an environmentally conscious electric vehicle now or goes on foot, after becoming Cosmos and leaving all his worldly possessions behind.

Did I steal the truck? Not exactly, considering I had a key. Plus, I had to get my belongings here somehow, and the lease on my sensible sedan was up. If Cole, er, Cosmos, misses it, I'll gladly give back the gas guzzler. Though by the heaps of snow around here, four-wheel drive will probably come in handy.

Holding my breath as I maneuver the truck through the narrow passage between buildings, I emerge into what was advertised as a delightful courtyard perfect for gathering. Is solid cement considered welcoming? Several other vehicles park haphazardly amidst banks of snow.

I check and double-check that I have the right address. Yup and yup.

Keep calm. Carry on.

Those words got me through a friendship that went south during high school, my mother going home to Italy afterward, a tricky junior year in college, undesirable living conditions, and of course, the breakup with Cole.

They're like a mental tattoo that I turn to when I'm not sure what to do other than hope and pray.

With a scratch of my head (this hat with the pom pom is getting itchy), I get out of the truck. A splintered bed frame rests next to a dumpster, a rusty bicycle leans against a wall with a questionable red stain, and a lopsided stack of cinderblocks looks like it could topple over any second.

No one gathers, not even the landlord who I'm supposed to meet.

Glancing at the time, he's five minutes late, but maybe I'm in the wrong place. I pace a loop around the parking area and bristle at the sight of several broken windows. A plastic bag takes flight like a kite. I manage to get ahold of it and toss it in the dumpster.

If I'm in the right place, it isn't as advertised.

Shivering, I wrap my arms around my shoulders. A cloud passes overhead. The day was all sunshine and now dreary weather rolls in. Kind of like my life lately.

Then again, I've left all that behind and am ready to start fresh.

A man with a plaid shirt and work boots emerges from a door that slams behind him. He glances at my truck as he gets in his old beater then spots me when I give a little wave.

I hurry over, careful not to slip and slide on the icy ground. "Hi, excuse me." I try not to sound timid and infuse my voice with friendly confidence when I ask the guy if I have the correct address. This seems like the kind of area my police officer brother would warm me to avoid.

"Ah, you'd be looking for Bill Krumpus. He's the landlord."

"Oh, so this is actually a residence? Is there an office or someplace I can find him?"

"He lives in unit 13 all the way at the end." The guy points to his left.

I nod as my stomach tightens with nerves because if he lives here, why is he late for our meeting? What if the apartment isn't available? And I don't have a place to live? I came all this way. Like the clouds gathering overhead, my excitement dims. "Great. Thank you." Taking a deep breath, I remind myself that I survived living in an apartment in college with six other people that was in a shady part of Seattle. Then again, Dominic made me move out and into a safer neighborhood after he came to visit.

But I can handle this.

Keep calm. Carry on.

After knocking lightly on the door to number thirteen, no one answers. I try again and then a third time before heavy footfalls approach. The door swings open to reveal a man with a scraggly beard, sallow skin, dark eyes, and a sharp nose.

I check my watch. "Hello, I'm Gloria Cardellini. We spoke on the phone about me renting one of your units. We had a meeting about ten minutes ago."

He grunts.

"Number four." A tremor builds inside because one, I don't exactly want this to be the place I'm going to live. Two, I already signed a contract and gave a down payment but also because affordable options in Hawk Ridge Hollow are slim. Three, I don't know where else I'd go.

He grunts again.

Fear gives way to confusion. "I mailed you the paperwork, the down payment, and called two weeks ago to confirm."

Another grunt.

Yes, the man is terrifying, but he mostly used full sentences on the phone. Also, a crumb in his beard distracts me. Is it a sesame seed? A breadcrumb? Not shiny enough to be a banana... And each of his grunts instead of a verbal reply like a normal human being ratchets up my irritation.

"Sir, am I in the right place? Are you the landlord? Uh, Mr. Krumpus?" More like grumpus, but I keep a friendly smile plastered on my lips.

"Yeah. Hang on." He slams the door, stomps around, there's a thud, then he returns with a key. "Go through that door, down the hall, and you'll find number four on the right." He gestures vaguely behind me.

"Um, okay." I hold up the bag of cookies. "These are for you. Thank you and Merry Christmas."

He grunts, but we make the trade nonetheless, making me an official Hawk Ridge Hollow resident.

With a careful skip in my step—because of the ice—I cross the parking lot. The main door squeaks when I open it and something scampers away. A cat? I hope so. The hallway smells like damp carpet, bug spray, and seafood. The floor creaks and someone chatters indistinctly from behind number six. I wonder if I should consider these as warning signs.

Go back while you still can!

When I reach the door with a number four painted crudely on the metal, I envision the photos I saw on the listing of a studio-style space with a brick wall, kitchenette, and sunshine spilling through the large windows. As I slide the key into the lock, I say a prayer.

The door opens, and I exhale.

It could be worse. Yes, there is a black plastic trash bag in the corner, a few leaves breeze across the floor when I set my bag down, and crumbs litter the counter, but the windows aren't broken, nothing drips from the ceiling, and I leave the gross smells behind me in the hallway.

I came this far. I can do this. Keep calm. Carry on, er, in this case, carry boxes and bags in from the truck.

After bringing everything inside a space that gives off abandoned factory vibes and is the perfect candidate for my favorite HLTV show, Designed to Last. My phone trills with a call.

"Hi, Domino," I say, using one of many nicknames for my brother.

"Hey, Gloria. You get there okay?"

"Sure did. I can see why Dad loved Hawk Ridge Hollow so much."

After our father passed away, bereft with grief, our mother never spoke about him again. However, Dominic talked about him every chance he got, including stories our father told about coming here and camping in the summer and skiing in the winter. I was too young to remember much more than the sound of his voice. Dom tells the stories to keep Dad's memory alive.

"I'm looking forward to visiting you there. So how's the new place?" my brother asks.

"It's, um, cozy." Before he can threaten to come out here and build me a place to live or do some other outrageous thing that his overprotective mind conjures, I add, "It's smaller than it looked in the photos."

He goes on a diatribe about how we should've come out last month when he had time off work, how renting sight unseen is dangerous, and asking if there are smoke alarms. "I already contacted Captain Hawkins to inspect the place for hazards and to make sure the CO_2 detectors are properly installed. You have to be careful with old buildings like that. He'll be by sometime next week. Expect a call."

"Dom, you reached out to the fire chief?"

"Just as a precaution. You can never be too careful. After that last bullet you dodged—"

"Dommy, I'm not the one who dodges bullets—"

We both go quiet because the expression hits close to home, to a tender place in our hearts where we keep our father safe. Dad was a police officer who served with courage and kindness. But he was shot while on the job. Ironically, Dominic also became a police officer, much to our mother's chagrin. However, she returned to Italy the week after I finished high school and didn't even see him graduate from the academy.

"Just saying, you dodged a bullet with Cole." Dominic's tone sharpens when he says my ex's name.

"I don't think he was going to cause me to experience carbon monoxide poisoning."

"Gloria, he was not the kind of man who'd take care of you. Who'd check the batteries in the smoke detectors once a year. To keep supplies for storms. To be sure your car tires were properly inflated. To make sure you don't wander off a ledge if you sleepwalk."

"I haven't done that in a while."

"That you know of. You live alone."

"Fair point."

"For example, was he prepared for the power outage a couple of winters ago? No, he wasn't. That's not the kind of guy you want in your life."

My brother isn't wrong, but I can take care of myself. I have to. I proved myself during that outage by bringing Cole bottles of water when he ran out. I also provided him with extra blankets, as well as candles.

We wrap up the call with Dominic's promise to visit in a few weeks. I cannot wait to show him around the place Dad dreamed of taking our family.

***

After two days of unpacking and settling in, I test outfits for my big day at my new job tomorrow. I'd hoped to get a spot in the accounting department at the resort, but they weren't hiring. Not yet.

I consider this position at a small business in Hawk Ridge Hollow as a stepping stone. It's an opportunity to get to know the area and people. That way, I can strategically position myself as an ideal job candidate when one opens at the resort. According to their website, they have great benefits, a solid retirement plan, and free lift tickets.

My phone beeps with a notification from an app called EyeDate. Signing up for it goes against every code of safety my brother makes me promise to adhere to. But a few months ago, my best friend Libby thought it would be a good idea to get me out of what she dubbed my "Cole Canyon." It was like a slump but deeper.

That's to say, being blindsided by him like that didn't do my ego any good—no pun intended. EyeDate is a play on words because it's a blind dating app. The

About Section" explains that the "Eye" part, when said out loud, sounds like "I", as in *I date*, or "i" as in the techy prefix for things like cellphones. Go figure.

Libby filled in the information for my profile and the app sends alerts with a little chime when it matches you with someone in your area.

Anyway, I went on all of one blind date using EyeDate and it was a flop. Not only was the guy late, he left abruptly, saying he had to walk his dog. This was immediately after his phone pinged with a notification. One I soon realized is the universal EyeDate chime for new hits.

Oh, and he ate all of my French fries when I went to the bathroom.

Le sigh.

I ignore my phone because I'm no longer in Spokane. When it pings three more times, I open it to check the settings. Turns out, it updated my location and sent me notifications from a few local Hawk Ridge Hollow guys. Let's hope Mr. Krumpus isn't into online blind dating.

Because I'm alone and have unpacked and organized everything, I have a look at the man market in Hawk Ridge Hollow.

The first one is a self-described bachelor for life. *Skip*.

The second is just a string of emojis. *No thanks*.

The third consists of a quote from a horror movie. *Hard pass.*

The fourth contains information for most of the personal fields: six feet tall, brown hair, gray eyes, employed in finance. There's also a quote from The Office. It's my favorite show, so I tap to chat only to see if only to get my geek on for a moment. I'm necessarily looking to date but wouldn't say no to a fellow Dunder Mifflinite.

EyeDate provides a few ice breaker questions before it

allows you to exchange messages. His answers are pretty normal. At least there aren't any red flags.

If you could have a superpower, what would it be? **To fly.**

At least he didn't say X-Ray vision.

Where would you celebrate your dream birthday party? **Italy.**

I've always wanted to visit the place my mother and grandparents call home.

If you were to create a reality TV show, what would it be about? **My siblings.**

When we get through the questions, a prompt asks me if I'd like to proceed to a regular chat with "Bryan." If that's his real name. You can never be too sure about these things. At least, that's what my brother's voice of caution says in my head. Also, there's the whole Cole-Cosmos thing.

I make a gagging face. Then again, I'm the one using a dating app on a Sunday night, and he's probably off with the bendy-pretzel-yoga lady in Bali or someplace exotic.

The text bubble blinks, indicating Bryan is typing.

Bryan: Hi. I don't usually do this but am new in town. Figured this might be a way to get to know people.

Me: Same. Where are you from?

Meeting people on the app seems like a good enough excuse to talk to another person—the extent of my human interaction for the last few days has been retail exchanges and a few grunts from Mr. Krumpus.

Bryan: New York City. Moved here for work.

Me: Same. Well, not the New York part. Washington state. I start work tomorrow. Thinking of an Office binge to prepare. Real talk: Do you actually like the Office? Some people just say that because they think it's the right or cool answer.

Bryan: If liking the Office is wrong, I don't want to be Dwight.

I actually laugh out loud.

Me: Lol. Good one!

Bryan: I'm heading over to the Hawk & Whistle for dinner in about forty-five minutes. Want to meet?

Whoa. He got right to the point. Then again, this is the fast-paced world of internet dating, and from what the locals have told me, the Hawk & Whistle has amazing bread. I check my purse for the pepper spray Dominic makes me keep on hand.

Me: Sure. See you there.

Bryan: Great. Then it's a blind date. I'll be the guy with the glasses. Wink wink.

I think of Santa winking at Mrs. Claus, and my heart goes pitter-patter. After a quick, albeit cool shower, something I'll have to talk to Mr. Krumpus about because the water temperature only seems to be getting colder by the day, I put on a dark green skirt with tiny white polka dots, an off-white fitted sweater, and add my cutest pair of ankle boots.

Inching the truck out of the narrow passage between the brick buildings is an exercise in precision, but once I'm out, I head into town.

In less than ten minutes, I emerge from the winter wasteland of the industrial area and onto the festive main street where shoppers enter and exit the stores with gift bags in hand and the colorful lights in the town square twinkle. The ones on the massive tree in the center aren't yet lit. I bet Hawk Ridge Hollow has a big ceremony like at Rockefeller Center in New York City. I turn up the music and bounce along as I sing the familiar tune.

At the reminder of the city, Bryan floats into my mind. I wonder what he looks like aside from being tall with brown hair and gray eyes. Oh, and he said he's wearing glasses.

I hope he's not an ogre. Please, don't be an ogre.

I'm well past the rebound stage after the breakup with Cole, but after everything that happened with him, do I want to date again? Yes, except not an ogre and not a guy like my ex. I take a deep breath.

Keep calm. Carry on.

With a hopeful little skip that this might be fun, I enter the Hawk & Whistle Pub. The light is dim. Well-worn paths line the wooden floor. Old black and white photos of people cover one wall. A bar with a polished brass rail lines the other. Tables fill the center with booths on the perimeter.

I wait at the podium until one of the servers, dressed in black pants with a green and gold Hawk & Whistle T-shirt on top, comes over. A pregnant woman enters on a gust of cold air and waits behind me.

I gesture she goes first.

She waves her hand dismissively. "Oh, don't mind me. Just had a Bannock Bread craving. This kid can't decide if she wants the cinnamon sugar-covered kind they have in the morning or the cheese-covered one in the evening. I usually just opt for both. During my second pregnancy, I couldn't stomach the stuff. Go figure." She pats her belly.

"Hey, Frankie," the server says. "Your bread will be right out." She turns to me with a smile.

"Hi, table for two, please. A booth would be preferable." I glance around then lower my voice slightly. "It's a blind date."

Both women make an, "Ooh" sound.

My stomach jumps and my cheeks shade pink. "I've never really done anything like this before, but I'm new in town. So I thought it would be a good way to meet people. You know—" I wave my hand dismissively.

The pregnant lady says, "Good luck. Most women in Hawk Ridge Hollow don't need it. There's something about this place that draws couples together. The women I know find great guys. If only it worked the other way around. FYI: I have four single brothers if this blind date doesn't work out." She winks, grabs her bread from another server, and leaves.

I go to the booth and settle in, not sure what to do with my hands. Table? Lap? Spread across the back of the booth. No, no, and no.

I wait. Then wait some more.

Bryan is over fifteen minutes late.

I drink water, nibble the cheesy Bannock bread the server brought over, and study the menu. Another one sails by with a ceramic dish filled with bubbly, cheesy spinach and artichoke dip. When she checks on me, I order one for myself. She convinces me to also get the bacon-wrapped tater tots special with maple mustard dipping sauce.

Looks like Bryan is a no-show, and there's no sense going home hungry.

After my appetizers come, I dig in, not realizing the bacon would be molten, scalding my mouth. I wave my hand and chug water then glance up. A clean-shaven man with high cheekbones, a Roman nose with a little hitch in the middle, and no glasses hovers by the table.

My heart pitter-patters as his charcoal-gray eyes capture mine in a smolder that is part Rebel Without a Cause James Dean and all handsome Italian man with lips that could kiss a woman swoony.

Keep Reading…

ACKNOWLEDGMENTS

A sweet (and buttery) thank you to all the Ellie Hall Sweet & Swoony Fiction Fans Facebook Group who shared their favorite pies, who chat, comment, and help make writing a sweet and swoon romance a joy!

ALSO BY ELLIE HALL

♥All books are clean and wholesome, Christian faith-friendly and without mature content but filled with swoony kisses and happily ever afters. Books are listed under series in recommended reading order. ♥

-select titles available in audiobook, paperback, hardcover, and large print-

♥

The Only Us Sweet Billionaire Series

Only Christmas with a Billionaire Novella (Book .5)

Only a Date with a Billionaire (Book 1)

Only a Kiss with a Billionaire (Book 2)

Only a Night with a Billionaire (Book 3)

Only Forever with a Billionaire (Book 4)

Only Love with a Billionaire (Book 5)

The Only Us Sweet Billionaire series box set (books 2-5) + a bonus scene!

Hawkins Family Small Town Romance Series

Second Chance in Hawk Ridge Hollow (Book 1)

Finding Forever in Hawk Ridge Hollow (Book 2)

Coming Home to Hawk Ridge (Book 3)

Falling in Love in Hawk Ridge Hollow (Book 4)

Christmas in Hawk Ridge Hollow (Book 5)

The Hawk Ridge Hollow Series Complete Collection Box Set (books 1-5)

♥

The Blue Bay Beach Reads Romance Series

Summer with a Marine (Book 1)

Summer with a Rock Star (Book 2)

Summer with a Billionaire (Book 3)

Summer with the Cowboy (Book 4)

Summer with the Carpenter (Book 5)

Summer with the Doctor (Book 6)

Books 1-3 Box Set

Books 4-6 Box Set

Forever in Love and Laughter

To Swoon or Not to Swoon over the Billionaire

To Love or Not to Love the Billionaire

To Crush On or Not to Crush On the Billionaire

To Date or Not to Date the Billionaire

Christmas Do Over with the Billionaire

Ritchie Ranch Clean Cowboy Romance Series

Rustling the Cowboy's Heart (Book 1)

Lassoing the Cowboy's Heart (Book 2)

Trusting the Cowboy's Heart (Book 3)

Kissing the Christmas Cowboy (Book 4)

Loving the Cowboy's Heart (Book 5)

Wrangling the Cowboy's Heart (Book 6)

Charming the Cowboy's Heart (Book 7)

Saving the Cowboy's Heart (Book 8)

Ritchie Ranch Romance Books 1-4 Box Set

♥

Falling into Happily Ever After Rom Com

An Unwanted Love Story

An Unexpected Love Story

An Unlikely Love Story

An Accidental Love Story

An Impossible Love Story

An Unconventional Christmas Love Story

♥

Forever Marriage Match Romantic Comedy Series

Dare to Love My Grumpy Boss

Dare to Love the Guy Next Door

Dare to Love My Fake Husband

Dare to Love the Guy I Hate

Dare to Love My Best Friend

♥

Home Sweet Home Series

Mr. and Mrs. Fix It Find Love

Designing Happily Ever After

The DIY Kissing Project

The True Romance Renovation: Christmas Edition

Extreme Heart Makeover

Building What's Meant to Be

♥

The Costa Brothers Cozy Christmas Comfort Romance Series

Tommy & Merry and the 12 Days of Christmas

Bruno & Gloria and the 5 Golden Rings

Luca & Ivy and the 4 Calling Birds

Gio & Joy and the 3 French Hens

Paulo & Noella and the 2 Turtle Doves

Nico & Hope and the Partridge in the Pear Tree

♥

Visit her website www.elliehallauthor.com for more.

♥

If you love my books, please leave a review at your favorite retailer's website! Thank you!

xox

ABOUT THE AUTHOR

Ellie Hall is a USA Today bestselling author. If only that meant she could wear a tiara and get away with it ;) She loves puppies, books, and the ocean. Writing sweet romance with lots of firsts and fizzy feels brings her joy. Oh, and chocolate chip cookies are her fave.

Ellie believes in dreaming big, working hard, and lazy Sunday afternoons spent with her family and dog in gratitude for God's grace.

facebook.com/elliehallauthor
instagram.com/elliehallauthor
bookbub.com/authors/ellie-hall

LET'S CONNECT

Do you love sweet, swoony romance?

Stories with happy endings?

Falling in love?

Please subscribe to my newsletter to receive updates about my latest books, exclusive extras, deals, and other fun and sparkly things, including my FREE short story *New Year with a Billionaire*, a sweet romance!

Get your copy at www.elliehallauthor.com

Facebook @elliehallauthor

♥

Printed in Great Britain
by Amazon